The Unprofessional Photographer

Ratinder Jhaj

First published in India 2010 by **Frog Books**
an imprint of **Leadstart Publishing Pvt Ltd**
1 Level, Trade Centre
Bandra Kurla Complex
Bandra (East) Mumbai 400 051 India
Telephone: +91-22-40700804
Fax: +91-22-40700800
Email: info@leadstartcorp.com
www.leadstartcorp.com / www.frogbooks.net

Marketing Office:
Unit: 122 / Building B/2
First Floor, Near Wadala RTO
Wadala (East) Mumbai 400 037 India
Phone: +91-22-24046887

US Office:
Axis Corp, 7845 E Oakbrook Circle
Madison, WI 53717 USA

Copyright @ Ratinder Jhaj

All rights reserved. No part of this publication may be reproduced, stored in or introduced into a retrieval system, or transmitted, in any form, or by any means (electronic, mechanical, photocopying, recording or otherwise) without the prior written permission of the publisher. Any person who does any unauthorised act in relation to this publication may be liable to criminal prosecution and civil claims for damages.

ISBN No: 978-93-80154-27-5

Publisher and Managing Editor: Sunil K Poolani
Books Editor: Monideepa Sahu
Design Editor: Mishta Roy

Typeset in Book Antiqua
Printed at Repro India Ltd, Mumbai

Price – India: Rs 125; Elsewhere: US $12

for the two boys in my life –
my husband and my son –
who let me spend so much time in front of the computer

About the Author

Ratinder Jhaj is a clinical pharmacologist involved in medical teaching and research for the last fifteen years. She has several national and international publications in her field, but this is her first foray into literary fiction.

She is currently based in Pondicherry, India, where she lives with her husband and young son, and works as an associate professor of pharmacology in a government medical college.

She can contacted at: balarati@hotmail.com

PROLOGUE

Monday,
August 25, 2008
2:45 am

There were only three images.

One showed a patient on a hospital bed. A doctor was injecting a drug into his intravenous line. Nothing out of the ordinary. Except that the patient was or had a striking resemblance to Kabir, and the physician was or looked remarkably like Naina.

The second image showed Naina drawing a drug from a vial into a hypodermic needle.

The third shot was a close-up of the vial. The label read Refludan, a brand name for the anticoagulant drug, Lepirudin. Extracted from the saliva of the medicinal leach, Lepirudin is a blood thinner preventing clot formation in the veins. It is especially recommended in patients whose platelet counts fall due to the more commonly used Heparins. Nothing remarkable. Except that Kabir had died of an intracranial hemorrhage or bleeding inside the brain, the most dreaded complication of any anticoagulant including Lepirudin.

There was no accompanying text. There was no need. The message was clear. Someone was trying to tell me Naina had killed him. But wait! What am I talking about?

Who are Naina and Kabir?

To cut a long story short... Actually, if you bear with me as we go back a few years, I'd rather tell you the long version. ❖

CHAPTER 1

Saturday
July 7, 2001

The day I first met Naina, I slept with her. In the doctors' duty room of Christian Medical College, Ludhiana. It was my first emergency room duty as a general surgery junior resident.

Things were going pretty cool. There had been only two surgical cases till 1am.

The first was a sixty something babaji with a bulge in his left groin which worsened on coughing. Clinical examination revealed the cause to be an inguinal hernia or protrusion of intestines through a weak area in the abdominal wall. Both symptom and disease had obviously been present since months if not years ago. But the old chap had waited till tonight to come to the hospital. His idea of an after-dinner stroll perhaps. He had walked into the emergency room accompanied by a crowd of relatives of various ages. I could have sent him home and asked him to report to the OPD or out patient department next morning. But he seemed so disappointed at the suggestion, that I admitted him and sent him to the ward. He would be evaluated at rounds tomorrow morning and I would be taken to task for taking him in.

The other case came in just after midnight. This time it was a younger male somewhere in his early twenties with a gash in his scalp. He had had a peg or two of the local brew and gone to sleep on a charpoy on the terrace of his house. Some time during the night he had got up and gone to the edge of the terrace to empty his bladder ; not an uncommon practice if you had a vacant plot of land next to your terrace. But in his inebriated state, he had missed the end of the parapet-less roof and tumbled down.

He was lucky to escape with just a scalp wound and a few bruises. After losing his balance, he seemed to have gained his sobriety. I didn't think he merited an emergency neurosurgery consultation. That could wait till morning. So I stitched up his scalp and placed him under observation. For long we remembered him as the piddler on the roof.

An hour after midnight, I decided to get some shuteye. After asking the casualty medical officer and the nurse to keep an eye on my patient, I headed for the duty room. This was a room within the emergency area with two bunk beds, a sofa and a TV. Five people could sleep here at a time provided the TV was off or you were too tired to let it come between you and your sleep.

I climbed up on one of the upper bunks and fell asleep. When I woke up, it was 6 O'clock in the morning. I had slept a straight five hours. Not bad for an emergency night. As I climbed down from the bunk, I noticed another doctor on the opposite lower bed. She was sitting at the edge of the bed combing her hair. There must have been other staff coming in and out of the duty room to catch some sleep during the night, but at the moment it was just the two of us. Nothing extraordinary in a doctor's night life.

"Are you an intern?" she asked as she finished capturing her hair into a pony.

"No ma'am, I'm a JR." I was not sure if she was senior to me, but it was safer to err on the respectful side.

"Which department?"

"General surgery."

"July batch?"

"Yes." I decided to quit calling her ma'am.

"Only nurses and lady doctors use this duty room. The

guys sleep in the one next to the blood bank." This was right across the emergency room door, but no-one had bothered to inform me.

"Oh. I'm sorry. Nobody told me"

As she walked towards the exit, she was gracious enough to turn back, smile and add, "It's OK. No big deal. But remember that in future, or you may get into trouble, especially with the nurses."

She didn't introduce herself, but I learnt later that her name was Naina Bedi. Specializing in pediatrics, she was a first year junior resident like me. But unlike me, she had graduated from CMC so knew her way around better.

Kabir Goraya was my neighbor in the junior doctors' hostel or JDH, a four story structure right next to the hospital building and home to over a hundred residents at any given time. It had both single rooms and 'married quarters,' which were nothing but two single rooms joined together with the bathroom of one converted into a kitchen.

I first saw him at the PG counseling. A tall, clean-shaven or 'cut-surd' with grey eyes, typically sharp Punjabi features, and an athletic build which, I was to discover, was a gift of the genes and not the gym, he did not look like any of us bespectacled, lightly built male doctors. I assumed he must have accompanied a friend or relative. But he was there to enroll for MCh in plastic surgery after having completed MS general surgery.

Soon I discovered that his room was two doors from mine on the third floor of JDH.

He would often leave his door open and as I passed by, I would see him immersed in what I guessed correctly to be Fundamental Techniques of Plastic Surgery by McGregor.

One evening I knocked at his door. Perhaps he was new to the place like me and wouldn't mind striking a friendship.

"Am I disturbing you?"

"No. It's OK. Tell me."

"I'm Tara. Tarachand Sharma. First year general surgery."

Realizing that I was not going to go away from the door, he invited me in and gave me a chair. Since there was only one in the room, he sat on the bed. It was a surprisingly tidy room, quite unexpected for a bachelor's digs, with the bed made and no dirty clothes lying about except for the white overall hanging on the back of the chair which looked rarely used. The only cluttered spot was the study table covered with books, journals, suture samples, CDs. But here too, I could spot no cup with a layer of dried tea or coffee at the bottom or dirty plate with leftover sauce in a corner. Well now you know what my own room in JDH was like.

"I spotted you at the counseling. Plastic, right? Where did you do your MS?" I began by way of starting some conversation rolling.

"MBBS, MS, everything here. Feels like I've been in CMC all my life. And you?"

"Indira Gandhi Medical College, Shimla. I came in through the All India quota."

"Was surgery your first choice?"

"I was keen on ortho, but I'm cool with surgery too."

I didn't tell him that in January I had joined orthopedics in BJ Medical College, Ahmedabad. Two nights later, while returning to my room after attending a casualty call, I was waylaid by some knife-wielding goondas. They advised me to avoid dying young by discontinuing my PG and leaving Ahmedabad. Back in the male residents' hostel, a local resident revealed their interest in my departure, an interest well known enough to be called an open secret. An MLA's son was first on the waiting list for MS orthopedics. If I quit, he would get the seat. Now I understood why the professor and head of orthopedics had dilly-dallied in accepting my joining report. I had been to his office thrice a day for the past two days. Every time his secretary would tell me he was either in the operating theatre or in a meeting. I had requested her to keep my letter and hand it over to him. But she had insisted on my seeing him in person. I had been surprised at the keenness to meet me personally, especially when I learnt that at least two of my four batch-mates had submitted theirs' through the secretary. I didn't bother to report to him or the police. I left. Without a trace. Literally.

"Which unit are you in?" Kabir brought me back to the present.

"Red." There were three units in surgery; red, blue and green, each headed by a different consultant with an interest in a particular surgical branch. Red unit handled breast and endocrine surgeries, blue specialized in colorectal, while laparoscopies were the domain of green unit.

"Dr. Manoj Singh," Kabir named the head of red unit with a wry grin. "He's all right. Just loves to punish tall guys by keeping the operation table lower than he has to." Since Dr. Singh barely touched the 5 feet 2 inches mark, this was pretty low. "Don't make the mistake of asking him to raise it."

I already had and he had nearly chopped my fingers off the retractor. Another piece of information which my general surgery seniors had failed to provide me. I guess they believed in learning by doing.

Kabir went on to give me more useful insights into the quirks of the surgeons and anesthetists, whom we surgeons are destined to work closely with, to watch out for.

From then on, I became an everyday nuisance, dropping into his room and joining his gang of friends and co-surgeons for meals in the JDH mess.

During one such dinner, Naina joined us. Of course she remembered me from our encounter in the ER. She teased me and insisted I had blushed and stammered like a schoolboy caught in the lady teachers' staff room.

She was Kabir's girlfriend. They were 'fixed up,' which means they were going steady in CMC terminology, ever since she was a fresher and he a third year MBBS student. During ragging, a group of rowdy seniors had wanted her to dance on one of the college canteen tables. A common enough demand, but when they began to insist she do an item number, Kabir had intervened. I don't claim to know much about the female psyche, but such an act of gallantry from an attractive senior does not often go unrewarded. And it didn't.

Naina and Kabir. Even their names sounded good together. I used to tease Kabir that he should take up her surname after marriage. That would make him Kabir Bedi, the handsome though now ancient hunk of Bollywood.

Chaaya. Chaaya Susan Masih. We called her Chaaya Memsahib

She was my first girlfriend. In fact, my only girlfriend. She was... Well, she was Chaaya. Slothful and a workaholic, sloppy and neat, brash and gentle. Her day began sometime after eight in the morning, often in response to a frantic SMS from her intern to rush to the ward just in time to be ready for the morning rounds. It was the residents' duty to check on the patients, look up new reports which had come in during the night, before the consultant came for rounds, usually at 8:45am. In her haste, she would often turn up in a mismatched salwar-kameez. But that, I guess, is chic nowadays. Anything goes by way of a salwar suit. Short kurtis with salwars (bottom halves are called salwars, right?), and long kurtas with jeans. I see girls in churidars without dupattas, and I see girls in jeans wearing one. Wonder what happened to the graceful punjabi suit? Anyway, to get back to Chaaya, she looked good in whatever she threw on. Mehendi-tinted curls fell, her nonchalance didn't stop at her clothes, into dark eyes, beautiful by themselves and helped not a little by long eyelashes and kaajal. At 5' 6,"she appeared nearly as tall as my 5'10." Somehow girls do look taller than guys of the same height.

She would enter JDH mess and call out "*Oye Pappu, ek khana, ek chai,*" one meal and one tea. It did not matter that the mess boy's name was not Pappu. She could watch anything that happened to be showing on the mess television, a movie, a match, NDTV, for exactly ten minutes or as long as her meal lasted, with such interest and enthusiasm you would think nothing could pull her away. Meal over, it was as if a switch went off in her head, and she was just as eager to get back to the obstetrics and gynecology wards or labor room.

Once in her department, Chaaya was a different person.

The outside world ceased to exist for her. I had to sometimes literally pull her out of there. Brash as she could occasionally be, with her patients she was patient and gentle. She liked to call them ranis or queens.

Only once did I witness her losing her cool with a patient, or rather a patient's husband. We were approaching ward 19, the gynecology ward, when a decently dressed, seemingly literate man accosted us. "Sister..." he began, addressing Chaaya. A nurse happened to be passing by with a dressing trolley. Chaaya stopped the gentleman in mid-sentence, pointed out the nurse and said, "You see that lady in a uniform? She is the one you want."

"No, no. I meant... *aap meri bahin jaisi hain*." He was quick to change his track and tone.

"Look, I am not your sister and Raksha Bandhan is six months away. So please don't waste my time."

"Sorry, Doctor. Actually I'm with the patient on bed number 8. I wanted to know..." He finally got the point.

I met Chaaya through Naina. They were batch-mates and best pals from college days.

"Tara?" Unlike her more reticent friends, Chaaya had not hidden her amusement at the effeminate first half of my name, which is how everyone addresses me. Almost everyone.

The third time I met her, she plotted our first dinner date. She made me lay a wager over something silly. I think it was an India-Pakistan one day. Oops, my apologies to all cricket fans. The loser had to treat the winner to dinner at Gazebo, a restaurant downtown. Very smart! It did not matter who won or lost. Either way you dined out together. Many more dates followed that first one. All I remember is that we laughed a lot. Something you were bound to do, with a little sense of humor and Chaaya thrown together.

So within a month of joining my residency at CMC, I had two friends and a girlfriend. Quite unusual, really. It's more common for medical PGs to finish three years of residency without knowing the name of the fellow next door.❖

Friday
January 23, 2004
11:45 am

We were by now in the final throes of our post graduation with only months to go before the qualifying examination. I had just finished checking on yesterday's post-operative cases. I thought of stopping by at the labor room to see if Chaaya was free for a bite at the hospital cafeteria. But as soon as I stepped into the ground floor corridor leading to LR, I knew something was amiss. A throng had gathered at the LR door, peeping in through the two transparent circles in the frosted glass. Inside there was another ring of people in the narrow passage, which opens on to the passive and active labor areas and the delivery rooms.

At the centre of this group was Raana, a ward attendant. He was alternately shouting threatening obscenities and pleading for the return of something. The object of his desire was his cell phone, now with Sister Ruth, the nurse in charge of LR. Called 'Ruthless' behind her sizeable back, she was the one person Raana dared not try his strength on. Naina and several of the LR staff, doctors, interns and nurses, were also there. A few of the obstetrics patients stood nearby clutching their enlarged bellies and glaring at Raana. What was up?

This is how Naina described it to me later:

An expectant mother was about to deliver, so a pediatrician had been summoned to receive the baby. Though another resident was on LR duty, Naina had volunteered to come because she knew Chaaya would be there. When she arrived, the patient had not yet been taken to the delivery room. Chaaya was doing a pelvic examination on her. Instead of going back, Naina decided to wait at the nurses' station from where she had a view of most of the LR.

There were 25 beds in the LR, but today only eight were occupied. Except for Naina and Sister Ruth, everyone was engrossed in either assisting Chaaya or watching another patient whose pains seemed to be coming on frequently.

Each LR bed has curtains which can be closed when a patient needs privacy. From where she sat, Naina suddenly noticed a pair of dirty men's shoes and trouser ends below the curtain hem of one of the beds. This was directly opposite the one on which Chaaya was examining her patient. There was something unnatural about those still feet. Was there a patient on that bed? Did the feet belong to a husband who was not supposed to be here? Naina quietly got up, approached the bed and pulled aside the curtain, expecting to find a husband who had stayed beyond visiting hours. Instead she found Raana, a ward boy. There was no patient on the bed. He was so startled that something fell out of his hand. His cell phone. Had he been making a clandestine phone call? What a place! Surely he could have found more private spots.

Both bent to pick it up, but Naina managed to get at it first. She was about to hand it over, when she noticed the phone's camera was on. She drew her hand back just as Raana lunged to grab it from her. It fell down for the second time. By now the rest of the labor room staff were upon them and the patients were getting quite excited over the commotion. To prevent further disturbance and any premature labor, the party proceeded towards LR door with Raana close on their heels. That's when I came in.

From where he had been standing, Raana was facing the foot end of the opposite bed. That was where Chaaya was doing the pelvic exam, the patient lying exposed. I need not explain what part of her anatomy was in view. Though the curtains around the bed were drawn, they were opened every now and then as someone came in; a nurse fetching an amniohook, an intern coming in to see what's happening, another bored and leaving. These were the moments Raana waited for, camera phone in hand. Cell phones with camera were still a luxury back then, priced in five figures. His could shoot videos too. How and why was a ward attendant able to afford it? Now we were to find out.

Someone opened the images on the confiscated phone. A deathly silence fell on the group. Even Raana, who had all this time been screaming and demanding his phone, stood suddenly silent as the cat came out of the phone. There were images after images of women in various states of undress. And the sickening fact was that they were not porn artistes engaged in erotic activities. These were patients being examined by doctors; expectant mothers changing from street clothes into hospital gowns, newly delivered mothers breast-feeding their babies.

The video gallery was filled with the same disgusting stuff in action. Last was the unfinished clip of Chaaya's patient undergoing a pelvic examination.

Who would find this stimulating? Plenty, apparently. Even as the confiscated phone was thus being explored, an SMS arrived in the inbox. "Any new maal?" That's what the sender wanted to know. It was quite clear to all of us what maal was referred to here. There were many more such enquiries in the inbox. There were also messages quoting certain amounts in rupees. Price for these clips? Was this what it was all about? Violating the dignity of these hapless patients for a few rupees?

Somewhere in his thirties, Raana alias Randeep Kakkar worked as a ward attendant or helper to the ward nurse, pushing patient trolleys, providing bed pans, getting drugs from the pharmacy, instrument packs from central sterile supply etc. He was known for his 'weakness' for gynecology and labor wards. He was often found hanging around there no matter where else he was posted in the hospital. In retrospect, this should have rung a bell in someone's head. But his cheerful willingness to fetch countless cups of tea and samosas from the canteen besides fulfilling his ward duties, had him safely placed in the good books of the nurses and doctors. I, for one, had never given him much thought till today.

Today his dastardly act got him nearly killed by the patients' relatives.

Tall Punjabi hunks had gathered at the LR door, demanding to know what was happening. Were their women safe? What exactly had this badmash been doing?

Had they been able to lay their hands on Raana, they would have beaten him senseless, or more likely, lifeless. Thankfully, they were pacified by Dr. Sarla Kaul, the obstetrics and gynaecology head, and some of the other senior faculty who had arrived at the scene by then. They were persuaded, not very truthfully, that he had not been successful in his outrageous endeavors. Ignoring his pleas to settle the matter within the ward, and his protests that *we* were violating *his* privacy by going through the contents of his cell phone, Raana was marched to the medical superintendent's office by Sister Ruth, Naina and Dr. Kaul. The MS assured everyone he would call in the police and make sure this heinous act in his hospital did not go unpunished. We had no reason to doubt him.

Saturday
Jan 31, 2004
8:15 pm

"Hi guys!" Naina smiled, throwing her stethoscope and white coat on an empty chair and taking another one.

Kabir's original research paper on reconstructive surgery in leprosy had been accepted for publication in the International Journal of Leprology, Venereology and Dermatology. This called for a treat at Gazebo or City Heart. But Naina was on call tonight, so we settled for dinner at the hospital cafeteria. We would make him take us out some other night. Anyway, it had been a busy week and we looked forward to a foursome chat, even if it happened over oily parathas and butter chicken. It was still a welcome change from the JDH mess.

"How are things at PICU (pediatric intensive care unit)?"

"Not so good. Our babies are growing microbes like culture plates. We have three cases of neonatal septicemia and two of meningitis who are simply not responding to antibiotics. We've tried everything we have; imipenem, linezolid. Hospital infection control team paid us a visit in the morning. That freaked out Chopri. And you know she de-stresses by screaming at one of us. Today it was my turn. She began evening rounds by giving me a dressing-down because our intern didn't pick up the culture and sensitivity reports."

Dr. Sangeeta Chopra was the head of unit one in pediatrics. Not a bad soul. But she did tend to get worked up when things were hectic. Which, unfortunately for her subordinates, happened most of the time in our pediatrics department.

"Where's Chaaya? I thought she'll be out of Labor Room by six."

"She's probably bringing another brat into this world right now. She had a primi lined up in the afternoon. So you know it could take a while," I updated her. "Talk of the devil and here she is," teased Kabir, who was facing the café door as Chaaya entered. But he didn't receive the usual bang on the head with Williams Obstetrics.

"What's wrong, Chaaya?" Sobriety from Chaaya meant all was not 'in the well' as she liked to put it.

"Guess who came to see me today? Manjot and her husband." Chaaya could barely wait to sit before she began.

Manjot was the patient Chaaya had been examining when Naina caught Raana shooting with his camera phone.

"At the time Manjot did not seem overly upset. Guess she was preoccupied with her new baby. Today she came back with her husband. He said she has been behaving strangely. Last night he found her crying by herself. She keeps thinking about what that bitch filmed. Every time she breastfeeds her baby or goes for a bath she has this feeling that someone is watching her. She insists he stand at the door to make sure no-one is watching. They again wanted to know exactly what happened last Friday."

"Oh my God! Poor lady. How could we expect her to go home and simply forget about the whole episode?" Naina was all sympathy. "What did you tell them?"

"What I've been told to. Dr. Sarla Kaul had called a meeting of all the OBG staff on Monday and briefed us on how to handle queries which were bound to arise after 'The Incident.' We were strictly tutored to say that Raana had not been successful in capturing Manjot on camera. No word was to be uttered about the other video clips. So that's what we have been telling our patients, including Manjot. But today I felt less than honest in saying what I did."

"But you know what, I think he only shot her a few seconds, and her face is not visible," recalled Naina, who had had the closest look at the damning material. "So in Manjot's case it may not be far from the truth to say he was not successful. No-one can recognize her."

"Imagine all those other patients who are unaware of how they have been violated! I wish I had seen the clips myself. I could have identified some of my patients." Chaaya had been busy delivering Manjot's baby even as the drama had unfolded in her ward.

"Then done what? Told them? What can they do now? Anyway, now that Raana has been caught, further circulation will be blocked," Kabir tried to rationalize.

"Yes. But have you thought of the clips and photographs that have already been sent out? Not just through the cell. He's sure to have uploaded them on a PC. Who knows since when this has been going on?"

"I've been wondering about it too. That is exactly why I agree with Kabir. It's better that others don't know. Ignorance is bliss."

"You're probably right, Tara. But how horrible! The very thought of it gives me the creeps," confessed Naina.

"Sometimes I wish I had taken out the SIM card and memory card from that creep's phone,"

"But the police need proof of his crime. Moreover, it would have been tampering with evidence."

"Anyway, let's forget about him. Sorry to spoil the celebration, Kabir. Congratulations on your first publication."

"Thanks Chaaya."

"So you are determined to work with leprosy patients instead of Bollywood stars?" Chaaya was back in form.

Kabir had a special interest in reconstructive surgery for correcting deformities due to leprosy. Chaaya was forever pulling his leg telling him he should move to Mumbai and concentrate on cosmetic surgery instead. "Who knows, with your looks you may even get an opportunity for a career change. One of your film-star clients may offer you an acting role."

"Thanks. But I have no wish to spend the rest of my life doing breast enlargements and liposuction. Or waiting to be picked up by Karan Johar."

"Just kidding. You know we appreciate your spirit. Only thing is, I worry about how you two are going to earn a living. Can't expect fat fees from your patients. And your would-be better half is forever doling out money for food and medicines to anyone who pretends to be poor."

"Don't worry, I'll make the rich ones pay twice as much. You're right. One of us has to make money," Naina assured her.

"How did you get interested in Hansen's disease, Kabir?" I asked, never having done so earlier.

"I'm not too sure myself. I think I was in the eighth, when my father got posted in Vizag. I visited the leper's colony with my school. I still remember those men and women with their lumpy faces, hands with missing fingers. But I did not swear to work for them there and then. Those were days I was still dreaming of enrolling in the Indian Army. It's only when I landed up in this profession, I realized the visit was not forgotten. Only buried. So here I am."

Kabir's father, like his grandfather and great-grandfather, had served in and retired from the Indian Army. Kabir was expected to live up to family tradition and don the uniform. But a family tragedy compelled him to serve his countrymen in a different manner.

"Can we talk of something else now, please?" Kabir never enjoyed being the topic of the day for too long.

"Yeah, your ears are turning red." Chaaya wouldn't let him off so easily.

This banter went on for a while till it was time for Naina to return to the PICU.

She finished her meal and left us to enjoy ours at a more leisurely pace. Watching her leave the café, Kabir's face froze. Following the direction of his stare, Chaaya and I were shocked to see the one man we had tried to forget not ten minutes ago. Raana! He was just entering the café as Naina was leaving. Answering a call on her mobile, Naina didn't see him. But he did not miss her. He paused at the entrance as he spotted her and then his gaze found us. Before we could recover from the shock, he was gone. But in that split second his eyes had turned back on Naina. And the look he gave her chilled me to the bone.

Monday
February 2, 2004
3:45 pm

"There's something called bail, you know," Dr. Sunil Joshi, Medical Superintendent of CMC, informed us.

It was the Monday after spotting Raana at the Cafeteria. We were gathered in the MS's office.

"You did hand him over to the police, didn't you Sir?" persisted Naina

"Do you doubt my word?"

"No Sir. Of course not. But Sir..."

"He's back inside the Hospital." Kabir finished the sentence for Naina.

"He was not seen in any of the wards, was he?"

"No Sir, I'm sure he went right out of the hospital

from the cafe." I could barely keep the sarcasm out of my voice.

After the initial shock of seeing him right there in the hospital café, Kabir and I had rushed after Raana. By the time we reached the corridor, he had vanished. The café is on the ground floor. Not fifty meters from it is a door that leads outside. He could've used that to lose himself among the crowd on the hospital grounds. Or he could have turned into one of the innumerable wards and corridors inside the hospital. He naturally knew his way around.

"You know the corridors of a hospital are more or less a thoroughfare. Hundreds of patients and their relatives visit each day besides the staff. I can't block the hospital gates."

No. Of course not. How would the patients come?

"At least we can prevent this one person from entering. We could paste his posters at all the entrances and instruct the security to forbid his entry." This practical suggestion from Kabir did not go down well with the MS. Formerly head of internal medicine, Dr. Joshi was an accomplished and much published professor. But administration is a different scrotal game altogether.

From the expression on his face, we expected to hear something like, 'Are you telling me how to do my job?' Instead, Dr. Joshi simply ignored the suggestion.

"Look, I have discussed with the Dean and Director and we have taken appropriate steps."

While the MS is in charge of running the hospital, the Dean looks after the undergraduate and postgraduate academics at the medical college. The Director has overall charge of the hospital as well as the college.

"Meanwhile, the case is with the police. Why don't you let them handle it? If they decide to set him free what can we do? Why are you taking it so personally?"

"So that when I tell my patients such a trespass will never take place again, I can look them in eye." (Well spoken, Chaaya.)

"Yes, yes, I understand your concern, Dr. Chaaya. And I specially appreciate your vigilance and bravery in tackling that crook, Dr. Naina."

Despite the compliment, we knew he was beginning to get irritated. And I didn't really blame him. CMC was suffering from an epidemic of lawsuits for negligence in patient care. At least three cases against surgeons alone had been filed in the last six months. Although a majority of these were a fall-out of an increasingly litigation-savvy public, they did not do the reputation of Brown Hospital, as the locals still called it, any good.

Nor would public knowledge of the LR episode help. It was a miracle that the incident had not found a place on newsprint yet. Or was it a good PR job?

"Look, I am telling you again, we have done what needed to be done. We don't want any adverse publicity for the hospital. Why don't you get on with your duties? Tara, Dr. Singh mentioned some problem with your thesis. Have you checked it out at the university?"

Topic successfully changed. Also a reminder that our degrees and hence our futures were to a very large and uncomfortable extent in the hands of 'higher authorities.'

My thesis acceptance should have come in by now but it hadn't. I had already made two trips all the way to Faridkot and visited the dissertation section of Baba Farid University.

"Yes Sir, I met the concerned clerk at the university and he told me one of the referees has yet to return the evaluation despite several reminders. They are going to send it to another referee." Thesis acceptance is a must before we take our PG exams. Any delay is a nightmare for a resident.

Later that evening:

"There's only one place to find out if he's bluffing. The police station," said Naina.

"You mean the one on Brown Road?" That was the Division No. 3 Police Station, barely half a kilometer from CMC.

"Isn't that the one to cover our area? That's where the police come from for our medico legal cases."

"There's no way you two girls are going there or to any other police station," Kabir put an end to the ladies' plans. "Anyway, what will it achieve? If we find no FIR has been filed against Raana there, the MS will claim to have done so at the headquarters. He can even directly ring up the DIG for all we know." This was little enough. Our knowledge of police matters could fit on the tip of a 26 gauge hypodermic needle. It would take me nearly five years to improve upon it.

"At least if we find he has filed an FIR, we'll know the hospital administration is taking the matter seriously," Chaaya persisted this time.

"OK memsahib, we'll go and do the detective work," I said. In any case, there was no harm in satisfying our curiosity. That's what I remember thinking at the time.

Thursday
February 5, 2004
2:30 pm

It was three days before Kabir and I could get out of our wards together and visit the Division No. 3 Police Station. I still don't know what we hoped to achieve. But we made the trip anyway. This was a first real visit to the police for both of us. I cannot deny being more than a little uncomfortable. But even this time, we were not to enter the hallowed portals. The sun was still bright and warm and there were three tables laid out in the spacious courtyard, two of which were a hubbub of activity even this late in the afternoon. We approached the one which was slightly apart from the others and possessed a single occupant. Contrary to our expectations, it was not some pot-bellied paan-chewing Inspector. Instead, we were pleasantly surprised to find a young and trim looking officer reading the Punjabi edition of Indian Express. We recognized him to be the officer who often visited CMC for the medico-legal cases. He introduced himself as Sub Inspector Sukhvinder Singh.

Sure enough, he had no clue about any complaint lodged by CMC.

"Nahin ji, aheja taan koi case nahin haiga." No such case had been filed, he informed us in Punjabi. Still, he

summoned one of his subordinates and instructed him to go through the recent FIRs.

Nothing.

The rest of the interview continued somewhat like this in Punjabi;

"What had the accused been caught doing?"

"Taking obscene photographs with a phone camera."

"Of someone related to you?"

"No, they were women patients at CMC."

"Oh, your patients?"

"No, actually they were in the labor room. We are surgeons."

"Did you two catch him?"

"No. A colleague of ours did."

"Did he harm any of you or threaten you?"

"No." We couldn't expect him to take us seriously, not that we were being taken seriously, if we told him about the look that Raana had directed at Naina at the café entrance.

He paused. We began to suspect he was enjoying his day's quota of entertainment at our expense. Had we complained to the hospital authorities? He asked.

We could say yes at last.

"But they haven't lodged an FIR. If they don't want to file a complaint we can't go after this man." Did we want to lodge an FIR?

We were not prepared for this. We looked uncertainly at each other, before Kabir said, "Yes why not?"

"Did we have any proof of the offence, like the phone in question?

No again.

Were any of the affected women willing to come forward?

No. Except one, they did not even know they had been video-taped. Later we learnt we could have still filed the FIR. Neither proof of the crime nor the victim is mandatory to do so. But our naivety had been so palpable.

"Doctor saab," he said finally, in a tone of friendly advice from one who knows what is best for greenhorns like us. "Why don't you leave these matters to your hospital authorities? *Tusin apne patient sambhalo.* You take care of your patients."

Wasn't that what we were trying to do here?

Take care of our patients' dignity?

Saturday
February 7, 2004
Sometime in the evening

"Are you going to tell them about us?"

Chaaya had been summoned by her parents to Meerut to be 'displayed,' that was the word she used, before a prospective groom.

"Indian parents! Why do they educate their daughters?"

"To run their clinics," I suggested unhelpfully.

Her parents, both obstetricians, owned and manned a maternity hospital in Meerut. Like the fate of many children of practicing clinicians in India, Chaaya's education was part of their long-term plan to prepare trained and trusted hands to take over the reins of the hospital from them. Fortunately, this was not an issue with Chaaya because she truly enjoyed what she did. But now the pressure had shifted to her personal life. No doubt the would-be son-in-law was an obstetrician or a pediatrician. Even more important, a Catholic.

"They still won't let their children make their own decisions. If I were a metric pass or fail, I would have been gratified to be any doctor's wife," she continued, ignoring my comment.

"Are you going to tell them about us?" I asked for the second time.

"I'll try, I'll try. I can't promise. You know how my father flies into a rage."

"No, I don't. Never had the pleasure of meeting him."

"And Mom will not take my side. Not that she is intimidated by him. She's just too lazy to have a viewpoint of her own," she continued without acknowledging my interruption.

"You have to bring it up sooner or later. Better now

than after all of you go through a wild groom chase. Why don't you relieve them of their troubles?"

"Relieve them? You think they will be relieved to know their only child wants to marry a Hindu? Arre, not even a Protestant will do. And Tarachand Sharma from Palampur? I can picture my Dad asking, 'Where is this Palampur? Do we have an atlas somewhere?'"

I didn't appreciate the projected derision, overt for my hometown and implied for my name. Meerut wasn't New York either. As for being called Tarachand, what's in a name anyway? But I didn't want to argue. I wanted to ask her what she planned to do. Did she care enough about me to stand her ground? Or was she willing to give me up without a fight? Instead I asked her when she wanted to go.

"I'll take the 5.45 train in the morning."

"Fine, I'll drop you at the station"

"No need, I'll take an auto"

"Don't be stupid. It'll still be dark and foggy. I'll pick you up at 5:15."

"OK, Tara. That's sweet of you. You are a gem."

Then why are you selling out? I felt like crying out after her.

Sunday
Feb 8, 2004
About 6:15 am

It wasn't dark any longer as I returned after dropping Chaaya off at the railway station. But the fog was thick and visibility still poor as I parked my second-hand Yamaha at the JDH parking lot. I had barely pocketed the key when I suddenly found myself facing Raana. He had a knife in his hand and three rough looking men by his side. Knife-wielding hooligans were becoming a recurrent theme in my life.

"*Kya* problem *hai tum log ko? Naukri to gayi, ab* police *chowki ke chakkar kyon kaat rahe ho*?" What is your problem? I've lost my job. Now why did you visit the police station?

I wish I could write that I did something brave this

time, like hitting him or at least spitting in his face. But the knife had not lost its paralyzing effect on me.

"Aur woh doctorni hai na, kya naam hai uska, Nina ya Naina. Usse bol do apne kaam se matlab rakhe. Heroine banne ka itna shauk hai to nangi filam ki heroine bana doonga." Tell that doctor friend of yours to mind her own business or I'll cast her in a blue film.

I overcame my paralysis at last and managed to punch him in the face.

The next instant...

I have no clue what happened after that. All I recall is waking up in the recovery room, a ward where all post-op patients are kept for close observation before being sent to their respective wards. I had been operated for stab injury of the abdomen, Raana's gift for our perseverance. Fortunately for me, the knife first struck the helmet which I had been holding and had instinctively used as a shield. After sliding off the helmet the knife did find my abdomen, but could not venture too deep. Still, not taking any chances, my fellow surgeons subjected me to a laprotomy, surgically opening my abdomen to make sure that my internal organs were intact. They were.

Another brave action we did not take was to decide to fight Raana and his cronies. No, we did not pledge revenge. We did not swear to fight unto death these voyeurs who were running lose within our hospital premises, a threat to the patients and now to us too.

After my encounter with Raana, I had debated about relaying his threat to Naina. In the end, I decided she had a right to know. So I told Naina and Kabir in as many of Raana's words as I could bring myself to repeat. Although shocked at his vengeance, Naina was raring to go after the man herself if need be. It fell to us men to suggest we quit playing Nancy Drew and Hardy Boys.

I cannot say that we had tried everything possible. But we had tried everything reasonably possible. We had approached the medical superintendent and been told to leave the case to the police. But no case had been made out. Hospital administrators did not want the matter to take the logical route to the police, law courts and from there to the media. They were too concerned about the hospital's image to take any legal action against an employee clicking nude images of their patients. So they simply fired the man and put this 'minor unfortunate business' behind them.

We had been to the police and were advised to let our hospital authorities tackle the matter. The police had gone a step further. They had informed the guilty about our interest in him. How else could Raana know about our trip to the police station? Our friend Sub Inspector Sukhvinder Singh was not so unique after all.

I had had one more meeting with him. With my stab injury, I had been a medico legal case. Sub Inspector Singh had visited my hospital bed to record my statement. Though Raana himself had not stabbed me, I had testified to his presence which made him an accomplice to crime. An FIR had been registered. But could we expect follow-up action against them? From the keeper of law who tipped off those who broke it?

What more could we have done?

We could have carried our complaint to higher police officials. We could have nagged the MS and perhaps forced him to take some real action this time. We could have approached one of the news channels who may have even run a 'sting operation.' Or we could have pursued what we were there to do, our PGs. Hospital bigwigs were not going to thank us for the unwanted publicity that would necessarily follow any earnest pursuit of the matter. Even if they did not turn vindictive, where was the time? Final examinations were barely three months away. We did have our studies to catch up with, cases to work up, seminars to present. We had to make a choice.

I confess without shame that we chose the latter. We decided to concentrate on our work, get our degrees, move out of Ludhiana, and carry on with our lives.❖

CHAPTER 3

That is what we did over the next year: got on with our lives till the day Naina called.

It was a Monday evening, the beginning of May, 2005.

"Haan, Bolo Kabir..."

"Hello, Chand. It's me." It was Naina, Mrs. Naina Goraya, making a call from Kabir's cell. Naina and Kabir had married a month after he finished his MCh and she completed her MD last June. Soon after the wedding, they had relocated to Chandigarh. Naina joined the Government Medical College as a lecturer, while Kabir became an assistant professor of plastic surgery in the Postgraduate Institute of Medical Sciences or PGI. We had remained in touch through phone, e-mail and a few trips to the Union Territory on my Yamaha.

"Oh! Hi Naina! Where's the rightful owner of the cell?"

"The rightful owner is admitted in Nehru Hospital, PGI.

"What! What happened?"

"Someone hit from behind when he was driving home from PGI last Friday. He had a long OT list, which got over some time after 7pm. He was driving home on his motorcycle when a gypsy banged into him from behind. Didn't stop, of course. He's fractured his femur. They operated on his leg that night itself, put in a nail."

"Why didn't you give me a call sooner, Naina?'

"Everything happened so fast that night. Saturday I thought of calling, but then I remembered you telling Kabir you were on call on the weekend of seventh and eighth." That was so typical of her, to think of a hundred excuses for not asking for help.

"So what? Big deal. I could have exchanged duty with someone. Anyway, how's he doing now? You want me to come? I'll drop a leave application with my batch-mate Suresh and start first thing in the morning."

"No, no. Things are under control now. Kabir's parents came in by the Shatabdi on Sunday. He should get discharged before the weekend. Come then, if you are not on duty again. It'll cheer him up."

"OK, will do that. But are you sure you don't want me to come right away?"

"No, really, there's no need. His parents are here. Plus his friends from PGI are pitching in. In fact one of them, one Dr. Sameer Mehta, you've probably met him at our place, has just taken Mummy and Daddy to the canteen for tea."

"Fine. But where's the patient? Give him the phone if he's around."

"He's sleeping. That's what he does all day, even after they've stopped his morphine. OK, Chand. I'll hang up now. Ortho is here for evening rounds. See you on the weekend. I'll let you know where to come, here or at home."

Naina had taken the lead and decided to call me 'Chand,' the nickname I wished to be known by. Loved to joke and laugh she did, but her jokes were seldom at other peoples' expense. So while many persisted in addressing me as Tara or even 'Twinkle Twinkle', she kept my preference in mind. And now I knew it was my convenience she was thinking of. So even as I clicked my phone shut, I decided to leave for Chandigarh at the earliest.

Saturday
May 14, 2005
3:30 pm

'Cum 2 pvt ward room 46 3rd floor'

From his SMS, I knew Kabir was still at PGI. Despite my best intentions of rushing to my injured friend's bedside, I had had to wait for the weekend. Suresh, whom I had relied upon to relieve me of my duties, was down with a viral fever, leaving CTVS short of hands.

I dismounted at the bus stand in Sector 22 and took an auto. With temperatures soaring to a record 43°C, I had chosen not to drive. After meandering through the unfamiliar corridors of Nehru Hospital, I knocked on room number 46, private ward.

"*Aao, aao beta.* How are you?" I was embraced by Kabir's father, who had opened the door. The Brigadier looked every bit a fauji, retired from service but not from an active life if his physique was anything to go by, unless it was constitutional like his son's. In any case he had definitely preserved himself well. Unlike Kabir, his father sported a turban, a pale blue one.

Next I found myself in the arms of his spouse. If the husband fitted a prototype, the wife was anything but. She was not your usual well-built Sardarni with long tresses, but small and petite with short hair cut in steps. She was the source of Kabir's grey eyes. We had met of course, on their trips to CMC and mine to NOIDA for their son's wedding. Both had the warmth of Punjab in addition to the social grace of a life in the Army.

Finally I approached my friend on the hospital bed. Other than his injured leg and a week-old stubble, he looked fine. In fact he seemed to have put on some weight.

"So, old chap, what does it feel like to be on the receiving end of the knife for a change? How many bones did you break? Wish I had done Ortho after all. Would have loved to fiddle with your bones," I teased.

"No thank you! Anyway, it's only my femur shaft which came under the bike. They've put in an intra-medullary nail."

"How come they haven't discharged you? The nurses don't want to let you go?"

I winked at his parents, who after their initial exuberance on seeing me, had retreated to their seats with that worried look peculiar to parents when their child's health is the issue.

"No *yaar*. They started me on Enoxaparin, for DVT prophylaxis." Deep vein thrombosis or formation of clots in the blood vessels is a dangerous complication of surgery. A small clot or embolus can dislodge from a larger thrombus and reach the lungs through the right side of the heart. Pulmonary embolism, as this condition is called, is the third leading cause of death in hospitalized patients.

Patients at moderate to high risk of developing DVT are given Heparin or one of the smaller particles called Low Molecular Weight Heparins (LMWHs), like Enoxaparin. Kabir fell into the moderate risk group.

"I was to be discharged. Naina could give me the injections at home, but then it seems I've got HIT. So from yesterday they switched to Lepirudin. Now they won't let me off till they are happy with my aPTT, " Kabir continued.

"HIT with Enoxaparin? That's pretty rare isn't it? I can't think of a single patient of ours who's had it."

HIT or Heparin Induced Thrombocytopenia, a decline in the blood platelets, is a complication more often seen with Heparin than with Enoxaparin. It is a serious condition, as it can paradoxically lead to DVT, gangrene of the limbs, even a stroke or a heart attack.

"Naina checked it out on the net. Incidence of HIT with LMWHs is 0.084%. Which means I'm the one in 1,189 patients who can develop it. Anyway, they've stopped Enoxaparin now. So tell me the latest from CMC. How's your MCh going? How's your MCh going? I heard your asshole of a boss left? Who's heading CTVS after him?"

Kabir still couldn't talk for long about himself. While the rest of our flock had flown the nest, I had stayed back to pursue an MCh in Cardiovascular and Thoracic Surgery in CMC.

"We have a new Professor, from Delhi. But before I forget, I got you something."

The latest Deff Lepard. Don't ask me how it is. Suresh recommended it." I did not share Kabir's enthusiasm for heavy metal or for much else in western music, except maybe The Beatles and Backstreet Boys. Small town guy, after all. "And a not so new Hemant Kumar for your wife. It'll help her relax after enduring your tantrums. By the way, where is she? Where's Naina?" I asked, handing over the CDs to Kabir.

"She's gone to buy Lepirudin. It's not available in the hospital pharmacy. She must have driven to Sector 15. This has been quite a strain on her, Tara. I'm worried for her. She needs to rest and take things easy, not run around looking after a limping husband."

It was four months since Naina was carrying their first child.

5:30pm

"After the rounds I'll go and drop Mummy and Daddy home. Why don't you also sleep at home tonight, Chand?" suggested Naina, "You must be tired after OPD and a two hour ride. You can spend all of Sunday here at the hospital."

We were waiting for Dr. Ratnesh Das and his orthopedics team to finish OT and come for evening rounds.

"I'll be fine. No problems. In fact you could do with some rest. I'll be with Kabir for the night. You can enjoy the luxury of your own bed tonight."

"Yeah, meanwhile we guys have a lot of catching up to do," seconded Kabir.

"I know what you want to catch hold of, Kabir. Tara, don't you go and get him a beer or something. If a nurse finds you enjoying hard drinks in the ward..."

"Beer is not a hard drink. It has only 4.8% alcohol."

"Now don't start that again Kabir. Tell me what else you needed from home besides clean bermudas."

"But seriously Naina, why don't you stay at home tonight?'

"No Chand, I'll simply fret there. I'd rather be here."

"OK, then at least let me drive Uncle and Aunty home."

Naina and Kabir had acquired a Santro after moving to Chandigarh. But Kabir's dad, after a life of being chauffeured in army jeeps and gypsies, was not confident of driving an unfamiliar car in an unfamiliar city although he drove a Zen in NOIDA.

7:00 pm

Evening rounds were over.

Naina had left to drop her in–laws home in the staff quarters of the Government College in Sector 32, about 10 km from PGI. She needed to fetch some clothes for herself as well as for Kabir, so she could not delegate the errand to me. Kabir and I had moved to the closed-in balcony which each private room had.

It had a small bed on which a patient's relative could sleep at night. Kabir was sitting on it with his left leg perched on a stool, while I pulled a chair from the room.

"Chaaya called..." Kabir started with the awkwardness which still accompanied the name of my ex-girlfriend Although Chaaya had rejected the 'suitable boy' lined up by her parents in Meerut last year, we ceased to be a couple the day she agreed to meet someone else. I was not prepared to keep my fingers crossed and continue to be her Mr. 'all right' till she found Mr. Right. Yet we had continued to be on affable terms, much to the confusion of Naina and Kabir, and leading them to hope that we would get back together.

That was till Chaaya finished her MD, left for the USA, cleared her USMLE Part III, started a residency, and found herself a husband, all within six months. Yes, Chaaya was married. To someone else. And no, he was not a catholic. Not even a Christian. Not even a doctor. I guess the distance made it easier to defy her parents. Or was it that I had not been good enough?

Anyway, I was surprisingly un-shattered and un-heart-broken, again to the confusion of my two good friends.

At least Chaaya had had the grace to let me know personally, first hand. She had called from Dallas sometime at the beginning of the year.

'Hello Tara. How are you doing?' A million miles could not diminish the verve in her voice.

'I have some news for you,' she continued as always before I could answer.

'I'm getting married in April, on the 25th.'

It was May now. They may be on their honeymoon, in Hawaii or Las Vegas or wherever one goes for a honeymoon after getting married in the USA.

'Hey! Congratulations! So, who is the unlucky guy?'

'You'll never guess.' She ignored the teasing. 'His name is S. Venkatadri.'

Venkat what? Now that didn't sound Christian.

'...but we call him Venky.'

That did. But then I could have been called Tarry or Tarex.

'He's working as a computer engineer at the Bioinstrumentation Centre of UT Southwestern.'

'Slow down, slow down girl. Now what is this UT Southwestern?'

'Southwestern Medical Centre is where I'm doing my residency, Tara.'

And UT is as in Union Territory?'

'Don't act so daft. UT stands for University of Texas. I know you are in a state of shock, Tara. I hope you don't have feelings for me still.'

'Don't flatter yourself memsahib. Anyway, jokes apart, I'm really happy for you. Do stay in touch Chaaya, and all the best. Take care.'

So Chaaya tied the knot last month. The wedding was organized and sponsored by Mr. Venky's parents. They must have been glad enough to find an Indian bride for their son. Chaaya's parents did not attend. I learnt these details from Naina and Kabir. After asking her to keep in touch, I took no pains on my part.

Next morning
6:30 am

When I woke up on the two easy chairs pulled together to serve as my bed, I found myself thoughtfully covered with a sheet. Who else but Naina, who had slept on the extra bed, must have done that for a fellow victim of the AC which had faithfully maintained the room at 22°C throughout the night. This was the only issue I had witnessed the two of them fight over after their union, the AC at 22°C. Naina found it too cold, while Kabir actually started to sweat if it was anything higher. I don't know what compromise they had reached in their bedroom, but here in the hospital room the patient was naturally the boss.

The night had been otherwise uneventful. We were disturbed only twice, once at midnight and then early in the morning at 4:00 am by the nurses who came to take Kabir's vitals.

I helped Kabir get down from the bed and hobble to the loo. "The pain bothering you? Want me to ask the nurse for a Voveran or something?" I observed Kabir's grimace did not desert him even after I had helped him back on the bed.

"It's just a headache. I'm tired of this place. Hope they let me off today."

"Let's see what Dr. Das thinks about it," Naina said.

"Here's the car key Chand," she continued. "You know the way from PGI? Just keep going straight till you cross sector 7 on your left and 19 on you right. Then turn right. Again go straight till you reach the Gurudwara on the right. Diagonally opposite is GMC. You can either go straight, then turn left or go left."

"I think he'll figure it out once he's in the area, Naina. He's not that dumb," Kabir interrupted her.

"Yeah, sorry. I wasn't thinking...I just..."

"It's OK. Relax Naina. I think you are too psyched out, managing a sick Sikh for the past week. That's what happens when you don't send for your friends. Now you sit and chat with your hubby and make his headache go away, while I make myself useful."

"Thanks Chand. In that case, if you don't mind, do one more thing for me. Pick up some bread on the way. Mummy can fix breakfast for the three of you. Sorry, you are going to be an errand boy today."

"At your service ma'am."

I was to drive to their house, have a wash and breakfast, and return with Kabir's parents.

It is both a pleasure and a pain to drive through Chandigarh. The pleasure lies in the wide, straight roads lined with beautiful trees, some with bright red flowers, others with yellow, although if you ask me the names of those flowers I wouldn't be able to help you, having no clue whatsoever myself. Problem with driving in Chandigarh is that it all looks the same to me, each sector a xerox of the other.

Anyway, with the help of Naina's directions and a multitude of signposts, I reached Sector 32 without much trouble. After convincing the guard at the gate that I posed no immediate security threat, I proceeded to house No. 1221-B on the second floor of the new senior lecturer's block.

Uncle and Aunty were up and ready, eager to head back to their son in the hospital. Yesterday was the first night since their arrival on Sunday, which they had spent away from him. As we ate our bread and omelets I sensed the effort the couple was making to appear light and cheerful.

"Is there some problem beta? What is this cytopenia?" Uncle finally asked me.

Thromboctytopenia, Enoxaparin, Lepirudin, Refludan HIT, DVT, a PTT. What a jungle of medical jargon, incomprehensible even to the literate. Maybe more so. The safai-waalah or the rickshaw-puller would not expect to understand anything other than when to swallow the pill and what not to eat with it, so there is no struggle to do so, no surfing the net late at night, getting more muddled than ever with the flood of information.

I explained some of the stuff as well as I could, not exactly an expert myself. When it comes to drug names, a surgeon never is.

"He'll be all right na beta?' Aunty placed her hand on my arm.

"Of course, Aunty! It's just a fracture. The doctors are being extra careful only because Kabir is PGI faculty."

"In our days, if you had a fracture the doctors fixed it, gave you some painkillers and antibiotics and sent you home till you went back to get the sutures removed."

"That's all that would have been done now too Uncle, if Kabir had fractured his arm. In case of leg fractures the chance of forming a clot in your veins is more. So they started a drug to prevent it. Kabir has had what you can call a reaction to the drug, but now that it has been stopped, he's going to be fine."

"What did I tell you, Harjeet? Tara is a doctor and Kabir's friend. He says there's no need to worry, so you stop fretting. *Dil chhota na kar.*"

The Brigadier pretended all his queries had been for the benefit of his wife.

To me he said, "Don't mind her beta. You know about Kabir's elder brother?"

I did. Their firstborn was a captain in the 57 Mountain Division, when it got posted to Sri Lanka as a part of the Indian Peace Keeping Force or IPKF. Kanwal was all of 24 years old and engaged to be married. The girl's father, a retired Major General, had offered to use his influence to stop his posting. But Kanwal had declined. He had in fact, politely but firmly forbidden his future father-in-law from using his influence to alter his career graph. His own father could have pulled some strings too, but didn't.

Some months later, Capt. Kanwaljeet Goraya's name entered the list of fatalities suffered by the Indian contingent in Sri Lanka. That was in 1989.

"At first, I'm not sure what upset me more, losing my brother or my future,' Kabir had once confided.

Kabir was a schoolboy, planning to follow family tradition into the defense forces. Cantonment life was the only life he had known. After the tragedy, his mother refused to risk sacrificing another son. Not wishing to grieve his parents further, Kabir had reluctantly allowed himself to be dissuaded.

"I resented my brother for forcing me to suddenly change track. At fifteen, I also blamed him for making it unseemly for me to be having fun with my friends. I was expected to be in mourning. Not that I didn't feel bad.

But Kanwal was nine years older, damn it. When I wanted to play hide and seek, he was already on to cricket. While I went to the movies to watch the cartoon strip, he was a Bruce Lee fan. By the time I was nine, he left home for college, then the Indian Military Academy. So when he passed away, how was I supposed to miss him? For many months the only tragedy for me was that my mother and I stopped attending parties; Raising Day party, CO's welcome party, farewell party, ladies night... Time heals all wounds, but for me it took time and maturity to feel the pain."

Later that unforgettable day:

"Excuse me, are you with Dr. Goraya in room number 46? He has been shifted to the ICU." A nurse stopped us as we passed the nurses station at the entrance to the private ward.

I waited outside the ICU after helping his parents to put on mask, cap and gown and see their son one at a time. Naina came out when she saw me through the glass doors.

"It's ICH, Chand." Intracranial Hemorrhage, or bleeding into the brain. One of the complications of any anti-coagulant is bleeding, and among all bleeds, the most dreaded is what Kabir had right now.

"Remember he complained of a headache? Soon after you left, he vomited. It was projectile. I called Dr. Das on his mobile. By then he seemed a bit disoriented and he had difficulty moving his right hand."

"CT Scan?"

"Yeah, they've done it. It's somewhere in his left cerebrum..." Her voice lost its steadiness, which she was taking great pains to maintain, at last.

"Don't worry, Naina. He'll be all right." I put my hand around her shoulders, assuring her of what I was not so sure myself. "But how, Naina? Weren't they monitoring his aPTT?"

aPTT or activated Partial Thromboplastin Time, is the lab test to help guide the dose of many blood thinners including Lepirudin. Basically it tells us how fast our blood clots after adding a substance called kaolin. Normally it takes 26 to 33 seconds. With anti-clotting drugs, it should take longer. That is aPTT should be prolonged 1.5 to 2.5 times the normal. Anything less puts you in danger of forming clots; anything more and you may bleed.

"It came back 4 times normal in the morning."

Oh. So there probably *had* been an overdose of Lepirudin. Or a safe dose had somehow led to a greater effect. There are so many factors which determine how a drug acts that there isn't always a straightforward answer.

"Have you eaten anything since we left in the morning? Why don't you sit down somewhere while I fetch something from the canteen?" I looked around but there was no place to sit. "Better you come with me to the canteen while Uncle and Aunty are with him."

But again it was impossible to make Naina leave Kabir's vicinity. So I got her some tea and biscuits and made her sit down in the nursing area of a ward where she consumed the only food that was to go into her mouth that day.

"I hope he doesn't have any residual deficits Chand," she said as she sipped the tea.

I remember it as the concern uppermost in my mind too. That Kabir might have to live with a weak or useless right arm and right leg, hemi-paresis or hemi-plegia. That he may not live at all, none of us had even dared to fear.

Anyone can stop a man's life, but no one his death;
a thousand doors open on to it.

Seneca, the Younger

Kabir's parents had forbidden him from joining the Armed Forces, afraid to lose him like they lost his elder brother. But neither their love and precaution, nor the experience and expertise of the team of super-specialists in one of India's premier medical institutes could prevent what fate was determined to accomplish.

According to clinical trials done so far, in 84 out of a

hundred thousand patients treated with low molecular weight Heparins, the platelet counts dip dangerously. Kabir was one of those 84. He could have been one of the 99,916 who don't get this complication, but he wasn't.

About thirty-five of every thousand patients given the high-dose Lepirudin have an intracranial hemorrhage. Kabir could have been among the 965 who don't bleed into their brains. But he bled.

After a major bleeding episode due to Lepirudin, twelve out of a thousand patients do not recover. Kabir could have been one of the 988 who do make it. But he didn't.

At 11:45 pm that night, we lost him.

I have no words to describe the grief, the enormity of the loss for those he left behind.

For the father, who had already lived through the anguish of lighting the funeral pyre of a son.

For the mother, once the proud matron of two, left childless; both seeds of her womb gone back to dust.

For the young wife, widowed while pregnant with her first child, not yet recovered from morning sickness, not yet decided what to call him if it was a boy, or her if it was a girl.

For the child who would never know a father.

I can only imagine their pain and grieve their loss. ❖

CHAPTER 4

Saturday
October 15, 2005
Sometime after noon

At this point in my narrative, my fingers falter at the keyboard. How do I continue, without being labeled an opportunist, a vulture scooping down for carrion, if not waiting for death itself?

It happened as I first held Naina's baby, hers and Kabir's.

It was a Saturday afternoon in October; warm, but with the promise of becoming cooler in the evening. After morning OPD, I had driven to Chandigarh to see Naina's newborn. When I arrived at her place, mother and child were sound asleep. Naina's mother-in law, Kabir's mother, had picked up the slumbering baby and put her in my arms. As I looked into the infant's face, I wished… I wished it was mine! Mine and Naina's. There! I've done it. I've put it down in black and white. A good friend not six months in his grave, and I was coveting his wife. Holding the child he did not see, wishing it was mine. What kind of a creep was I?

I still do not know when my feelings for Naina became other than friendly affection. Maybe it started when I saw her playing *'chidiya udd'* with one of her patients in the pediatrics ward. Kabir and I had been catching up on our reading at the hospital library till it closed at midnight. On our way back to JDH, Kabir had wanted to look up Naina, who was on night duty in the pediatrics ward. I offered to carry on and leave them to themselves.

"Come on, don't be silly. Anyway she may be either busy or asleep in the duty room," Kabir had reasoned. But we found Naina doing none of the above. She was perched on a bedside stool entertaining a ten year old with lymphoma who was too uncomfortable with his chemo to sleep. She had that special smile which she reserved for her patients. Many pediatricians fix a small teddy or some such toy to their stethoscope to distract a child when they wish to examine one. But Naina didn't need a decoy. All she had to do was turn on her smile and it seldom failed to charm the tiny sufferers. Like it charmed me that day.

Perhaps I was already in love with her the day she presented me a Benetton T- Shirt. She had surprised me one evening, appearing at my door with a pale mauve Benetton on her arm. Kabir was the intended beneficiary, but it turned out to be a size too small for him. Would I mind trying it on? She would be happy if I kept it instead. Handing me the T shirt, Naina turned her back. Did she expect me to change in her presence? It would have been no big deal. But I had felt unnaturally shy of pulling out one shirt and donning another in her presence. So I slipped into the bathroom.

When I emerged fully clothed again, the look of approval in Naina's eyes had caused a sudden thrill to run through me. She had been admiring the garment of course, but the pleasure of that brief moment of intimacy came back to me every time I donned her gift-by-default. Needless to say the mauve T shirt became a favorite with a guy who had not ventured beyond blues, grays and browns before.

Or maybe I lost my heart when I first saw her in a sari. Our college was hosting a maternal and child health CME or continued medical education program. Both the girls, one training to take care of the mother and the other to look after her child, attended. Academic sessions in the morning were followed by the usual dinner. On their way out, Chaaya and Naina dropped by Kabir's room, which by now was often cluttered with me and my books too. Naina had draped a black sari with a bright orange border. Her hair was left open and she was wearing light make-up. Both deviations from routine suited her very well. Chaaya was there too. She also wore a sari. It was blue. Or was it green?

Now Smriti, that was what the baby had been named, was two weeks old. I had roughly known Naina's expected date of delivery, but it was some days after the new arrival that I received the news, not from Naina but from Chaaya, who rang me up all the way from Dallas.

Chaaya? Chaaya! Had she known all this while? Is that why she had refused to marry me? Had paternal opposition been simply an excuse to opt out of a skewed relationship, a sort of love triangle, for which I was responsible without even being aware of it?

Had she not married against her family's wishes after all? Then why not me? As far as I know, she did not even attempt to make my suit acceptable to her family.

When I had first learnt of her union with a Tamil Brahmin whom she met in Dallas, I had silently accused her of not loving me enough to fight for me.

Maybe she knew *I* did not love *her* enough.

There had been signs and symptoms, but I never made the diagnosis. Or had I chosen not to? On her return from Meerut, she had found me in the private ward, recovering from my misadventure with Raana.

"Oh my god, Tara! You know, I had feared he would try to make us stop meddling in his case. But I thought he would simply threaten us. I never imagined he would really stoop to violence."

"Actually, I punched him first!"

"What! Are you mad? Taking on armed thugs like that! What made you do such a foolhardy thing?"

"I didn't react at first. To be honest I was too terrified

to move. Then Raana said something obscene about Naina, so I hit him without thinking."

She had been standing at the foot end of the bed, her eyes on my bedside medication chart. There was a clank as this suddenly freed itself from her hands. Only the fact that it was tied to the bed's railing prevented it from falling to the ground. Chaaya had seemed unduly perturbed by this minor lapse. Soon, she left with some excuse of preparing for grand rounds. I had not even asked her about her meeting with Mr. Possibly Right in Meerut. I couldn't understand her hasty departure. Or I didn't want to understand.

Then at Naina and Kabir's wedding. A whole gang from CMC, including the couples' batch mates from MBBS, Surgery and Pediatrics, had traveled to NOIDA for the reception. Between friends, there was the usual teasing and leg-pulling of the bride and groom. After downing a peg or two of the vodka-laced 'soft-drinks,' I too contributed to the banter.

"If only I had joined CMC earlier, I would have met Naina first and Kabir wouldn't have stood a chance with her," was one of the silly jokes I remember cracking.

Later, over ice cream and *gaajar ka halwa*, Chaaya had found me alone and said something like, 'We often say in jest what we dare not utter in earnest.' Nice quote. Wonder who said that? But what did she mean? Which joke was she talking about? She walked away without an explanation and I did not insist on one. Or was it that I didn't want to know?

Was Naina the real reason behind my friendship with Kabir? Was that why I hung around in his room, because she would drop in? Was I dating her best-friend to stay close to Naina? To be counted among her inner circle? I could not be such a lowly scheming scum of the earth. Or could I? Such were the demons in my neurons. Such was my confusion, my self-disgust and guilt at the time, that it led me to do something even more shameful. ❖

CHAPTER 5

Tuesday
August 21, 2007
Around 8 pm

"Hello Tara. Naina here."

The sound of her voice after so long had a positive chronotropic effect on my heart. What I mean to say is, it made my heart beat faster. It was nearly two years since I last saw her. After that day of self-discovery I could not gather the courage to face Naina; to talk to her as if nothing had changed between us, as if I did not find myself thinking about her at least once every single hour of however many hours there are in twenty-two months. It's not that I spent those months pining away for her. Nor did I live a saint's life. But being where I was, in the operation theatre, the wards, the corridors, JDH mess or hospital café of CMC, there was no escaping from memories of her.

I had long since shed the guilt. The timing had taken me by surprise, but I was no longer ashamed of my emotions. I did not even feel guilty about transferring my affections. I'm sure that had Chaaya not wavered, had she taken a stand against her parents to be with me, I would've been faithful to her not just in the physical sense. If my heart, bruised if not broken, did warm towards the one other girl I met and talked to almost daily, what was so shocking in it? She was engaged to another, you would say. Yes, but then fate removed that impediment too.

"Hello? Tara, are you there? " There was just a tiny hint of complaint in her voice.

Or was it the echo of my guilty conscience? I know I just told you I had got over that. But I had indeed ill-used Naina. Not by loving her but by abandoning her. After I met myself, I never met her again. I did ring her up maybe three times in two years. I remember doing so a couple of days before Kabir's first death, what a terribly irreversible word, anniversary. I wasn't sure if there was going to be *akhand paath* or something on his first *barsi;* if Naina would like me to come. I didn't want to ask, didn't know how to. So I waited for her to mention it, which she didn't. I also stayed in touch with her through e-mail, if forwarding the forwards I received can be called that. Not much of a communication except that you know you are on someone's mailing list.

But in two years I never made the less than two-hour trip to Chandigarh. She had not been just a girlfriend, fiancée, and then spouse of a good friend. She had been my friend too. And when she could have used some compassion and the proverbial shoulder to cry on, I had disappeared. All because I had lusted for her at the most vulnerable point in her life. That was the real wrong I did her.

"PGI has advertised for some assistant professor posts," she continued. "Ritu, my MBBS friend from CMC, has asked me to send an application form. So I was wondering if you need one too. There's a vacancy in Cardiothoracic. Are you interested?"

Interested? To be in the same town just a few minutes drive away from her? To be able to see her every single day? Was I interested?

"When did the ad come?" No hint in my voice that I was willing to move to any place in the world, just to be with her.

"Don't know. I didn't see it myself. At least a week ago, I think. Ritu spotted it in the Tribune. 31st is the last date for sending in your application."

"Why not? From what I've heard, PGI has a good plastics department. The academics are vigorous too. If it's not a bother send one for me Naina. I'll send you the application fees."

"Don't be silly Tara." This time the hurt was definitely present in her voice. A few hundred bucks had never been an issue with us before.

Sunday
September 2, 2007

An elderly lady in a blouse and skirt opened the door.

"Hello Mrs. Karin. I'm Tarachand." Resolving to be a better friend to Naina, I was in Chandigarh on my first free Sunday after she called. I recognized the well turned-out old dame, luckily recalled half her name, and wondered if Naina's aunt remembered me. We had met only twice before, at a wedding and a funeral.

"Yes, yes, come in. Kabir's friend from Ludhiana, right? Naina said you would be coming." She disappeared into one of the two bedrooms.

Aunt Yookarin was all the 'family' Naina had before she married Kabir. Naina's mother had met Ruchit Bedi, a Sikh Art teacher, at a teacher's conference in St. Jesus and Mary in New Delhi where she was working as a librarian. After a year of long distance courtship, she had joined him in Shillong much to the amazement of her friends. All the way to Meghalaya to marry a school teacher!

Ms. Yookarin, who was already a confirmed spinster back in 1970s, was the warden of the girls' hostel of Sherwood Residential School in Shillong. She knew Ruchit since his school days, which he had spent more in the company of paint and brush than his textbooks, and continued to do so as an art teacher. Ruchit's father, a Sikh who had come to Shillong on business, fallen in love with the hills and a Khasi girl, and shifted base from Amritsar, had been well into his forties before Ruchit was born. He could not wait for his son to grow up and take over his travel agency. When his sixty plus joints could not withstand the wet and the cold anymore, he handed over the reins of his business to his local friend and partner, before moving back to Punjab with his wife. So there had been no opposition when Ruchit followed his heart in the choice of his career or life-partner. An only son, Ruchit had stayed back in Sherwood Residential, where Ms. Yookarin donned the role of his local guardian and did not relinquish it even after he left for college to graduate and then returned to school as a faculty. When and how a girls' hostel warden became so fond of a little brat, none could say. When Ruchit married, Ms. Yookarin treated his young bride from Delhi more like one of her wards than like a librarian. Mother was soon replaced by daughter. Naina was barely four years old when her parents died in a road accident between Guwahati and Shillong. She had been in the car too but escaped any physical injury. Aunt Karin took the young orphan under her care. What about her blood relatives; grandparents, her 'real' uncles, aunts? Didn't they want the custody of their own flesh and blood?

I had never heard Naina speak of any and I never presumed to ask. 'Aunt' Yookarin had represented her family at Naina and Kabir's wedding.

Naina finally appeared. "Hi Tara. Sorry. I was giving Smriti a bath."

Did I ever say how beautiful she is? I cannot analyse her features and describe each in isolation. But there is a pleasing softness in her face. In fact more than the anatomy, it is her expressions that are beautiful. After all that life had taken away from her, I would not have been surprised to find a more hardened, bitter and joyless version of her old self. But her dark brown eyes had not lost their sparkle. Her lips seemed ready as always to curve up in a smile. When she does that, two tiny dimples appear on her cheeks, her whole face lights up and... I'm no good at this sort of thing.

For the first time I felt an awkwardness in our meeting, our conversation. I wondered if she sensed it too and it did not make it any easier. Fortunately there was two years of CMC news to catch up on.

What followed was a year of weekends. If someone were to ask me what I did during the week, I wouldn't be able to tell much more than that I repaired a few hearts, anatomically; helped to bypass the blocked arteries of a few more; sutured some blood vessels and so on. But I have vivid recollection of all the weekends, or rather alternate ones. Having got into the habit of seeing her again, it took a great deal of willpower not to visit her every single Sunday. But I did not wish to crowd into her life after being absent for so long. Every other Sunday I would drive down to Chandigarh provided neither of us was on call. I would start early on those days, managing to wake up by five am without the help of an alarm clock and reach in time for a late breakfast.

Most of those visits were chaperoned. Aunt Karin was in town for a couple of months. When she left, Kabir's parents came down from NOIDA. Or I should say their twenty years older versions did. Nothing ages faster than sorrow. The Brigadier's shoulders were a little less square, his back less erect. His wife smiled and talked sparingly, as if afraid to mention her sons' names by mistake, or anything to do with them. They would have liked Naina and Smriti to move to Delhi with them, but Naina didn't want to quit her job. After a lifetime of living in defense accommodation, the Gorayas too were not keen to leave the house they had saved for and dreamed about, and which they could finally call their own. So they divided their time between the two cities.

Third parties were welcome. They helped ease the formality which had crept up between us. After breakfast, while Naina and her aunt or mom-in-law went about the business of lunch, I would get down to spoiling Smriti. At least that is what Naina complained I was doing. But I guess she did not really mind. Who would grudge the child a little extra dose of pampering? Thankfully, she was growing up surrounded by love and indulgence, blissfully unaware of her and her family's loss. Aunt Karin claimed she was young Naina's duplicate. Her grandparents thought her eyes and nose took after of their son's. I don't know who she looked like, but here I go comparing after all. With her curly hair unlike her mother's straight mane and her big twinkling eyes, she was the prettiest little two-year-old I knew. By now our comradeship had progressed to the level where she would let me sit her on my lap, at least when her mother and maid weren't around.

Sometimes I chauffeured Naina's car and took her in-laws to the Gurudwara. After Kabir's death, Naina had never stepped into a house of worship. After lunch we would sit talking or playing cards. In winter we basked in the sun in their balcony, shelling peanuts and eating them. Sometimes I did find myself alone with Naina, but by then our comfort level in each other's company had recovered sufficiently. In the evening I would head back to base and wait for the next trip.

I never stayed overnight in Chandigarh, except on the day before my PGI interview. Then too I had planned to start early in the morning from Ludhiana. But it was Brig. Coraya who insisted I should not take a chance. What if my bike broke down or there was a road block and I missed my 11am interview? So I did sleep over, but not at Naina's. I wasn't ready for that yet. Instead I slept in ODH or old (refers to the age of the building, not its occupants) doctors' hostel, the male resident's hostel in PGI, with a batch-mate from Shimla.

I don't know how much longer life would have continued in this vein. ❖

Monday
July 7, 2008

'With reference to your interview on 12th March 2008, we are pleased to offer you the post of Assistant Professor in the Department Cardiovascular and Thoracic Surgery.'

It had taken nearly seven months from application to interview. It was another four after attending the interview, before I received my appointment letter from PGI, thanks to legal squabbles initiated by some disappointed candidates. But the day I received it, I gave the requisite one month's notice to be relieved from CMC, Ludhiana. Four weeks felt more like fity-two. After spending seven not unhappy years in CMC, suddenly a month seemed an eternity. Finally the day came when I quit for good and headed for Chandigarh.

One of the first things I did after settling down in my new department, number 64, second floor, K block, was to convince my sister to come down from Palampur. Taruni, yes she has a more contemporary name, as I point out to my parents whenever the injustice of being christened Tarachand wins over my 'what's in a name' attitude, had a lump in her breast. Hopefully it was just an abscess or fibro-adenoma, but I needed to be sure it was not a malignancy. She had visited me in CMC and been advised to get it removed surgically, but she never did. This time I was planning to chain her to the OT bed if I had to.

Dr. Manoj Singh, my former unit chief and guide from Ludhiana, was by now in PGI too and undertook to take charge of my sister. Surgical biopsy confirmed the happy news. Taruni did not have breast carcinoma. It was a benign growth capable of becoming malignant if left untreated. Dr. Singh scared her enough about the consequences of leaving the lump alone to make Taruni let herself be admitted one day prior to the lumpectomy.

Sunday
August 17, 2008
7:30 pm

"I assumed your mother was coming too. Otherwise I would have left Smriti with Neelam and stayed the night with you here." Naina was apologetic when she came to visit Taruni in the ward the evening before her surgery.

Neither of our parents had accompanied Taruni. My mother has a fear of hospitals. There must be a term for it, some phobia. She *had* traveled to Ludhiana with Taruni for her first breast work-up. But then too she never entered the hospital, limiting herself to my room in JDH. It had been Naina and Chaaya who had taken turns to be with my sister during her examination and biopsy. My father didn't make it for that either. In fact I don't recall when my parents last traveled together. Oh, they are a happily married couple, both retired after three decades of teaching in the Agricultural University of Palampur. The reason for the lack of synchrony in their travels is neither disinterest in their progeny nor marital discord but Diesel, our nine year old daschund. The last time they tried leaving him in the care of our cook, he didn't eat for four days. They never took a chance after that.

It was the first time after Kabir that Naina entered one of the private wards of Nehru Hospital. Her work did bring her to PGI now and then for pediatrics CMEs. But the pediatrics department of PGI, thankfully for her, boasted of a new and separate block.

"Thanks Naina, but you have your hands full with Smriti," I replied on Taruni's behalf. "Anyway it's only a lumpectomy. She's going to be discharged tomorrow evening."

"But I'm going to irritate him for a week after that," threatened my sister. Dr. Singh wanted her to wait for the lump and axillary lymph node histopathology report and for the surgical site to heal fully before undertaking the nine hours bus journey to Palampur. Otherwise she might be forced to return with wound infection or, god forbid, require another surgery.

"What are you going to do all day in Tara's room while he's at work? Why don't you come to my place instead after the surgery? You'll have Smriti and Neelam for company and I come home for lunch too." Neelam was Naina's house-help, who did most of the housework and took care of Smriti. She stayed with them and the child was quite attached to her.

"No, no, Naina, that'll be too much trouble," I pitched in.

"Don't listen to your brother Taruni."

Do sisters ever, I wondered.

"Decide for yourself." Naina gave Taruni a tender look and stroked her hand.

"Are you sure it's okay with you? I'm tempted." Taruni ignored my glare.

"It's decided then."

"Naina, are you sure?" I repeated Taruni's query when I accompanied her to her car.

"Look, Tara, one-way relationships never work. Do you think I don't know what's happening here?"

"What do you mean Naina?" Had my true feelings for her been obvious after all?

"I don't know why you stayed away at first. Maybe you were uncomfortable with my loss. Many people are. But for the past one year, you have devoted almost all your free weekends to Smriti and me. Do you think I believe you when you say it's because you have nothing better to do with your time? If you can do so much for your friend's family, can't I do this much for yours?" God!

She had me scared there. I was too dazed with relief that she was not referring to a more sinister motive, to argue with her.

"Besides, I do have vested interests in the arrangement. Smriti will have a new face around her."

"Well, if you are bent upon it, I am relieved to have Taruni off my back for a week," I managed to reply.

"Shame on you!" she retorted.

That was a good week. The week that Taruni stayed at Naina's. I had a valid excuse to visit Naina every day. For me that in itself was sufficient to make it good. I would pack something for dinner and carry it over after work, or we would order pizzas or my favorite *pav bhaaji* from Hot Millions. Taruni and Smriti hit it off well together. Smriti would let her change and feed her and allow other privileges which I was yet to enjoy. Naina and Taruni's acquaintance from CMC got an opportunity to develop into a friendship.

I even felt a wee bit envious when I sometimes found them deep in 'girl talk', oblivious to my presence. Naina must have missed that after Chaaya left for the States. Once you leave behind the bonds made in college it's rare to find that intimacy and comradeship again. Opportunities are fewer when one has a family and a job. I often wondered what it must be like for Naina to live where she was, surrounded by her colleagues with their families intact. Emotionally, it may have helped to move out of the home which she had shared with Kabir. But then the walled-in college campus was a safer and more convenient place to live in. After all it is often the practicalities that determine our choices. Such is life.

Anyway, for the first time since Kabir, I saw Naina lighten up and laugh, truly laugh. Not a forced smile so that others don't feel uncomfortable.

The day before Taruni was to leave with an all clear from Dr. Singh, we took her to Nek Chand's Rock Garden and Sukhna Lake. It was Smriti's first visit too. I got a ticket for the *shikara,* the only one to be had without standing in a queue.

"Three adults? My dear brother, when did I ever go on a boat?"

I had completely forgotten about this other phobia in my family, hydrophpbia. Taruni would never venture anywhere near a body of water, be it a river, a lake or even a pond. The sea is thankfully far from Palampur. To climb on board a boat was out of the question for her. Smriti on the other hand was all excited about going in one, so there was no turning back, even if it had to be without Taruni Aunty.

I got in first and helped Smriti in. Then I held my hand out for Naina. I had casually touched her several times during our days in Ludhiana. We had exchanged handshakes. We had rubbed shoulders while I had helped her with her patients, during our subsequent nights together in the emergency. I had sat close to her in crowded auto-rickshaws. But today, as she gave me her hand, I was unprepared for the tremor that shook mine. I avoided her eyes as I busied myself in finding a place to sit. This too did nothing to ease my discomfiture. The *Shikara* seat, like any *Shikara* seat, was more like a bed. I moved to sit on the small plank opposite it, but the boatman compelled me to join Naina and Smriti on the 'bed' for the sake of balance.

"Arre saab, wahan kahan baith rahen hain. Memsaab ke saath baitho. Nahin to naav damadol hoyegi. Waisi bhi woh gila hai."

So there we sat, a typical picture of a family on vacation. One sideways glance at Naina's face and I knew the embarrassment value of the situation had not escaped her either. It was only Smriti's excitement and childish prattle which salvaged the evening from being a total disaster.

"What are you waiting for?" Taruni asked when we were alone after dinner that night. For the first time, I was sleeping over at Naina's.

We were to leave early in the morning to drop Taruni at our aunt's, my mother's younger sister who lived in Pathankot. Taruni had exaggerated the beauty of the drive sufficiently to convince Naina to accompany us. After a short stay at Pathankot, Taruni would carry on to

Palampur, while Naina, Smriti and I would head back immediately.

"Excuse me?"

"You love her." It was not a question.

"What if I do? It's too soon after Kabir..."

"Too soon! Wasn't it the summer of 2005? That's more than three years ago, Tara."

True, albeit a bit ironical, this marital advice coming from my sister.

"But it's rather awkward, Taruni. If she does not reciprocate my affection it would be impossible to go on being just friends. I'm too scared to risk that."

"That's a risk you'll have to take. How long do you intend to carry on like this, anyway?"

"I don't know. She still seems so vulnerable. It doesn't feel fair to pop the question," I reasoned.

"Not vulnerable. She's lonely, Tara. And that's something you can remedy. Besides, I think she likes you. Why else would she spend so much time with you? Not caring about the gossip that I hope, my dear brother, you are aware you two must be generating."

"Maybe she's never given it a thought. Maybe she just thinks of me as a friend from college."

"Bull."

"Taruni!"

"And what about you, Tara? Wouldn't you like to get married, have kids of your own? The two of you are not getting any younger."

"Look who's talking." I immediately regretted giving in to the temptation to turn the tables on her. Not married and at twenty-eight quickly passing the eligible age to do so in small town India, Taruni was a cause of sleepless nights for my parents, particularly my mother. I don't know what gave her more cause for concern, that her daughter may be left without a life-partner or that she would be left with her daughter on her hands for the rest of her life. Not that Taruni had sworn to stay a spinster. But, having left for Shimla for higher studies like me and having finished her masters in computer applications, she found the eligible bachelors of Palampur quite ineligible.

Which wasn't true really. There were plenty of qualified young men in the university. But she worked freelance from our home PC, so they never had their chance with her.

"I am not lucky like you to find someone I can love. Someone I love so much as to devote all my time and thoughts."

"Taruni, I'm sorry, I didn't mean to hurt you. I always assumed you were not interested in marrying. I thought you were cool with being single."

"I am. I'd rather be single than marry for the sake of it. Anyway, you do as you please. Wait till as long as you feel decency demands. How long has it been going on, Tara? Were you by any chance infatuated with Naina while she was with Kabir? Is that why you broke up with Chaaya?Is that what is holding you back now? A guilty conscience?"

"I don't know, Taruni." Was all I could manage in reply to the sudden barrage of questions which followed my sister's insight into the confusion of my sentiments.

"You know we can't always control whom we are attracted to. If only you knew the number of married Professors I've had a crush on! Ma and Papa would have stopped my going to the University." I knew she was only trying to cheer me up.

" And I'm sorry. I didn't mean to imply that you should feel guilty even if you fancied her when you shouldn't have. As long as you haven't done anything you shouldn't have."

"Like what?"

"Like having an extra-marital affair!"

'You..." I hit her with one of the cushions from the swing on Naina's balcony, before she could run indoors, laughing. Little did we imagine that someone was soon to be accused of a more serious crime.

Sunday
August 24, 2008

I was by now the proud owner of a new Skoda. Why

did I need a car, and that too a big one? I had been happy on my trusty Yamaha bike. Not even to myself would I admit it was so that I could drive a certain lady and her daughter around. But this trip was to drive my sibling halfway, or more like two thirds of the way home.

The onward journey took a little over five hours, with the advantage of an early start. Expecting to be slowed by increasing traffic and decreasing light on our drive back, we could not spare much time in Pathankot. So, after enjoying a delicious lunch cooked by my mother's sister and bidding farewell to my own, we headed back.

It was a warm August noon. The windows were up, the AC was on. The inside of the car suddenly seemed very intimate without any actual physical contact. I was very careful to prevent that after the boat ride. But the accidental feel of her *dupatta* beneath my fingers as I shifted gears, Naina's hair falling on my shoulder as she leaned back to tuck the sleeping child in the rear seat; these kept my senses buzzing.

Then it began to rain, insulating us further from the outside world. After some attempt at casual conversation, we sat quietly in the car.

"So Naina, how are you doing?" I think it was the sense of closeness which gave me the courage to broach a subject I had steered away from till today.

"You mean like how am I after Kabir? I am quite all right Tara. At least I have her." She looked over her shoulder. "And I have friends like you." She gave me a tight little smile and looked away out the window.

When I saw the tear escape down her cheek, I put my foot on the brake. What a goose! Why did I start when the road needed my attention.

"I'm sorry Naina. I shouldn't have..."

"It's OK Tara. Really, I'm doing fine. At least through the day. Where's the time to even think? It's only at night, after Smriti goes to sleep and I find myself alone with the TV remote. That's when I begin to wonder what is so wrong with me that God, if there is one, doesn't wish me to have a family? How come he let me keep my daughter? When is he going to take her too?"

"Shhhh..." I finally put my hand on her shoulder. She turned to face me fully.

"No one Tara, except her," She looked again at the child. "I have absolutely no one to call family unless you count my in-laws. After my parents there was not a single relative who wanted me. Mamma's parents were divorced and cared neither for her nor for their grandchild. Papa's parents were too old, in their seventies. They couldn't look after a four year old, though it seems they did come to see me all the way from Amritsar now and then. But they too were gone before I was old enough to form any memories of them. 'Aunt' Yookarin is all the family I know."

I let her pour her heart out as the skies seemed to echo the turmoil within her. It was just as well we had stopped.

"For nine years I dreamt of marrying Kabir and of finally having a family. Ten months were all I got. As if someone up there said, '*Sorry! It was a mistake. Naina Bedi is not supposed to have a life.*'"

When we neared her flat, sometime after ten in the night, it was pitch dark. Black windows and missing streetlights indicated an unscheduled power-cut.

"Isn't Neelam at home?" I asked as Naina began groping for her house keys in her handbag.

"She took the day off to stay with some relation in Sector 7. Since we were going to be out all day, I let her go. She'll be back in the morning."

I carried Smriti upstairs while Naina unlocked the door in the glow from her mobile, and fetched the emergency light from the bedroom. Meanwhile Smriti woke up and began to howl for her milk bottle. She still needed it to go to sleep.

"You be with her while I get her milk," I offered. What would she have done if I had left from the door?

"You'll have to prepare it."

"OK. Tell me what to do."

Following her instructions, I poured some milk into a feeding bottle, poured it out again when she reminded me 'I told you to filter it', filtered it back in, micro-waved it for thirty seconds, 'Yes seconds, not minutes, Tara,' and fixed the nipple on.

"What are you going to do for dinner?" I asked as I handed her the bottle.

We should have eaten on the way, but food had been far from our minds then.

Smriti did not allow her to answer.

"What are you up to?" Naina was surprised to find me in her kitchen twenty minutes later. I had managed to locate two packets of Maggi masala noodles, which were now boiling with some tomatoes.

"Don't have anything to eat in my bachelor's den. You might get some too if you wash your face and be at the table in five minutes."

Dividing the Maggi onto two plates and topping each with eggs which Naina had fried, we sat down to an emergency-light dinner. After the customary compliments and surprise at my culinary abilities, if preparing two-minute Maggi in thirty minutes can be called that, she ate her share rather quietly.

"This past week just flew by, didn't it? I'm afraid to think how much I'm going to miss Taruni. So will Smriti. I don't remember when we last had so much fun. It was as if I forgot..." She stopped in mid sentence.

How I longed to hold her and comfort her. Tell her I loved her and would do anything to make her happy again if only she would let me. But of course I did nothing of the sort.

"It's OK to forget, Naina. You'll always remember Kabir. We all will. But now and then it's all right to forget that you are his widow. You have to let go. I won't say for Smriti's sake. For your sake too I think its time you lighten up a little. Have some fun. Go out more. With Smriti. With friends. Go for a movie, window-shopping, anything."

She didn't say anything and I felt embarrassed at the possibility of having said too much. Finally she got up and carried her plate to the kitchen. I followed her and dumped mine too in the sink for Neelam to wash the next morning.

"Thanks, Tara." She meant more than the meal. But she was thanking me and dismissing me at the same time.

Sleep was not a possibility that night. The picture of her as I left her, alone in her dark flat with not even the TV for company tonight, kept my neurons too active to sleep. Finally accepting defeat, I switched on my PC. Had a case to look into for the mortality meeting on Monday. Thought I'd check the mail first. What I saw in my inbox made sleep not just improbable but impossible. For many nights to come. ❖

CHAPTER 7

Monday
August 25, 2008
2:45 pm

I do not usually do it. I don't open mail from an unknown source. I delete it straight off. But tonight was not a usual night. I didn't know any rajeshsuri@yahoo.com. Yet I opened mail from him.

There were only three images.

One showed a patient on a hospital bed. A doctor was injecting a drug into his intravenous line. Nothing out of the ordinary. Except that the patient was or had a striking resemblance to Kabir. And the physician was or had a remarkable likeness to Naina.

The second image showed Naina drawing a drug from a vial into a hypodermic needle.

The third shot was a close-up of the vial. The label on the vial was legible. It read Refludan, a brand name for the anticoagulant drug Lepirudin. A recombinant form of Hirudin which is found in the saliva of the medicinal leach, Lepirudin is used as a blood thinner to prevent clot formation in the veins.

It is especially recommended in patients whose platelet counts fall due to the more commonly used Heparins. Again nothing remarkable. Except that Kabir had died of an intracranial hemorrhage, which is bleeding into the brain. The most dreaded complication of any anticoagulant including Lepirudin.

There was no accompanying text. There was no need. The message was clear.

Someone was trying to tell me that Naina had killed him.

As if to make sure that I had got the message from the first, I received another mail two days later. 'I know who killed Dr. Kabir. Dr.Naina is a murdress. She injected overdose of Lepirudine.' Poor spellings, but he didn't forget the Dr.'s

That weekend, Naina surprised me by dropping in with Smriti. Their first visit to my abode. It was nearly eight in the evening. She had made the trip to visit her friend from CMC, Ritu Kapoor, the one who was indirectly responsible for my being a PGI faculty and was herself an assistant professor in internal medicine.

Though PGI assistant professors are entitled to spacious flats, these are ten kilometers away in Manimajra. Hence some single souls like Ritu and I, who would anyway not know what to do with a larger flat, had opted to stay at the accommodation on campus meant for married residents. This consisted of an L-shaped room and a bathroom. One limb of the L served as an open kitchenette, dining and drawing space all rolled into one, while the other served as a bedroom. The only partition between the two was a curtain rod. The curtain itself was to be hung at the cost and effort of the occupant. I took no such trouble for a couple of months. But eventually I discovered it was simpler to drape than to keep my bed tidy.

So it was not any anxiety about the state of my living space that was reflected on my face on finding Naina at my doorstep. It was a quandary I had already gone through in the past, the dilemma of whether not to convey a threat to Naina. I had yet to tell her about the mails. This time I had decided to wait. But for how long?

She sensed my distraction and misinterpreted the cause for it. "I shouldn't have come in unannounced like this."

"Don't be silly Naina. Come in. How did you come?"

"Drove down."

"How are you planning to go back?"

"A chartered helicopter will land shortly on your rooftop and fly me home. What's wrong Tara? Obviously I will go back the way I came." Despite her reproach, I was happy to detect signs of her former spirit. She was dressed smartly too, in a short pink T-shirt and three-fourths. After Kabir's demise Naina had taken to wearing mostly conventional salwar kameez. If at all she wore jeans, it was with something long and loose on top. Today it was apparent it was her interest in dressing up which had been lost, not her figure.

"I don't want you to be driving around alone at night."

"Why not? It's not yet eight. I was not planning to stay for long anyway. But now I think I should just leave."

"No Naina. Wait. You are misunderstanding me completely."

"Then what's with you Tara? First you advise me to lighten up. Now you are sounding like my father-in-law."

I took my decision then. I took her by the hand and guided her to the table which served as my dining, study and computer table. She looked at me as I switched on the PC. While that came on I put on the TV, surfed for Pogo, Smriti's favorite channel, and settled her on my only comfortable piece of furniture, a well-worn bean bag. Finally I came back to Naina.

"Sorry to be a little theatrical. There's something I want you to see. But before you do, I want you to know that what it suggests is absolutely, totally absurd. Not to be taken seriously. What we need to find out is why and who is behind this."

Preamble over, I finally let her have a look at the mails.

Her reactions fluctuated. 'How come? Where was the camera? That's the private ward.' Bewilderment followed. 'What's the big deal? It's Lepirudin, not morphine.' Next came anger. 'What the hell? So I gave him his injections. They were kept in the room, in the refrigerator. That doesn't mean I…' Finally there was despair. She sat there alternately opening and closing the two mails till I put my hand on hers on the mouse and signed out.

"Isn't it enough that he is dead?" I heard her use that word with regard to Kabir for the first time.

I turned her chair ninety degrees and pulled a stool to sit in front of her."I told you Naina. No-one is going to take this seriously Naina."

"What if the police does? The court, the media, Kabir's parents?"

I didn't want to tell her so, but she was right. I too had considered our options. The logical thing to do would be to approach the police. They had cyber crime specialists in the forces these days. But I wasn't sure where things would go from there. Wouldn't they like to see the offending mail? What if someone decided to investigate the accusation? Not for a moment did I consider it anything but baseless. But the police? Kabir's parents? Wouldn't it be natural for them to investigate any suggestion of foul play in their son's demise? It would be unnatural for them *not* to do so, even if their beloved daughter-in-law, the mother of their only surviving flesh and blood, was the suspect.

What then? Police, court, media. The media. Wouldn't they just love this sensational piece in an otherwise un-happening Chandigarh. Where would that leave Naina? Not in prison. There was very little fear in my mind of that. But very likely in public memory. *Isn't that Dr. Naina Bedi?* She had not changed her surname for professional reasons. Even that may go against her. *The one who was accused of killing her husband.* Not many would remember the verdict. Some may not totally believe it; *she was let off, but...who knows?*

I was not even considering a guilty verdict.

And to what end? It would be worth the turmoil if the culprit could be apprehended. But if that didn't happen, it would be futile suffering.

"Who could be doing this? Why?"

"I have tried to trace the mail."

"Oh, can you do that?"

"Googled some sites which tell you how to go about it. There are loads of them actually. But all I could discover was that the mails originated from Chandigarh. Big help.

Naina, if you don't mind, I think we should Sameer into confidence." Sameer Mehta was in the same department as me. He had been a good friend to Kabir, a friendship that I had since inherited. His family was settled in Chandigarh and may have some local contacts who could help us. In any case I needed to unburden by confiding in someone. As events turned out, it *was* Sameer who helped us, although without being aware of it at the time.

"Do what you want, Tara. I don't care. I don't care what happens now. I thought I had lived through the worst, but there's obviously more for me."

Silent tears trickled down her cheeks. Tears which she had been forcing back for the sake of her child. But tears or not, I think children do sense when things are not quite right. Smriti was sitting quietly in front of the TV all this while, without laughing at Mr. Bean's pranks, without her usual, 'Mumma, Tara Uncle, look what he's doing' commentary.

"Why are you crying Mumma?" She finally came over to us and tried to climb on to Naina's lap. I took her in mine instead.

"Mumma is having a bad headache *beta. Chalo* my buttercup," that was her favourite power puff girl, "shall we see what Tara Uncle has in his fridge for his girlfriend?"

"Why did he wait three years?" It was a much calmer Naina whom I drove home. But definitely not calm enough for me to let her drive back with only her daughter and thoughts of Rajesh Suri for company. So I took over her car, stopped at the hospital for a quick dash to look up a post -op patient, and then we proceeded to drive to her side of the city. I could always catch an auto rickshaw back to PGI.

"He didn't have an address before. You don't work here, thank god. But I do. I've been here only a month, and my e-mail ID is pinned on notice boards all over PGI."

'Residents interested in participating in the Cardiovascular and Thoracic Surgery quiz may contact:

Dr. Tarachand Sharma.

Ph: 2601885, e-mail: taracs@gmail.com'

"Why send it to you?"

"That beats me, Naina." Except for when Kabir was admitted, and then when Taruni had her surgery, there had been few opportunities for anyone to spot us together in PGI. We usually met at Naina's place. Had someone followed me there?

"Do you remember Raana, the fellow who was clicking nude patients in the labor room?

"Are you asking me if I remember the man who stabbed me, or his pals did anyway?"

"Sorry…I ..."

"It's OK, but what about him? Are you thinking he may be the one?"

"Isn't it possible? We didn't see him after he attacked you, did we? Chaaya saw him once at the pharmacy but that was some years ago. Never after that. Maybe he's here in PGI."

"It's possible, but I thought his interest lay in female nudity."

"Yeah, but he's one person who knows our association goes back to Ludhiana. He may think of reaching me through you."

"Don't know. You may be right, Naina. But would a ward boy have sufficient knowledge of drugs to be able to link Kabir's brain hemorrhage with Lepirudin?"

"That does seem a bit far-fetched. But the nurses do know that Lepirudin may cause bleeding. Raana was always chatting with them. Maybe that's where he picked up his information."

This was plausible. In fact it was written in red on Kabir's bedside chart; 'On Lepirudin. Do Not give Intramuscular Injections.' Intramuscular injections may lead to a haematoma, a collection of blood in the tissue, in patients on any blood thinner. A competent nurse is aware of this potential complication. An inquisitive ward boy may learn as much too.

"Anyway, try not to think about the mails, Naina," I advised as we reached her place.

"Don't worry, my daughter won't let me." Smriti had

meanwhile dozed off in the back seat clutching her stuffed tortoise.

"Don't worry Naina," I reassured again, I don't know whom.

"We'll soon be laughing over the absurd mails."

That was not to happen for some time to come.

This time it was a 127 second video clip. Of me approaching Naina's Santro from the passenger side leaning at the window to say something, Naina looking up and smiling, our faces appearing too close, and finally me walking towards the steering. That was just three days ago, the day I dropped Naina and Smriti home from my place in PGI. The day I had shown her the first two mails. I had stopped for a while at the hospital to look up a patient whom I had operated upon that morning. The video was of me coming back to the car where Naina and Smriti had been waiting. It had been an innocent enough moment. But from the angle of the recording our faces did appear to be nearly touching. With very little imagination one could even insist we had exchanged a quick kiss, which we hadn't. It was obviously taken from the lawn that separates the arterial road that runs through PGI from the hospital. With a hedge, a few trees and bushes, it would have made an ideal spot for clandestine photography. Had he, whoever *he* was, chanced to be in the lawn at the right time or had he followed us from K block? He must know my residence by now. This was getting creepier by the day. ❖

It was exactly ten days since that first mail.

I waited for the elevator to take me down after supervising the transfer of the last patient on the plastics OT list to the recovery room.

I remember meeting and talking with one of my colleagues, though who it was or what we talked about I can't exactly recall. I just remember that as I stood there waiting, someone passed by in the corridor. Someone I caught only in my peripheral vision, but that was enough.

Naina was right. It was him. Raana, our friend from CMC, was the e-mailer. She had thought of him when she first saw the mail. I don't know why I hadn't done so myself. Clandestine photography inside the hospital *was* his forte. Only, with much better phone cameras, if that had been used this time round too, picture quality was in the 5 mega pixel range. Raana. It explained a lot. It explained the time lag between the photographs and the mail. Maybe he chanced to pass by room 46, saw Naina and Kabir, and got down to his old tricks waiting for something interesting to capture. Naina might well have been too engrossed to notice. Having done the shooting, he may not have had much use for it until Kabir passed away. That might have given him the idea to link the snaps with the death. But with Kabir gone, he had no one to send the mail to. He obviously didn't trace Naina to GMC.

Then I joined PGI, with my contact details pinned all over the notice boards.

Finally he had an address. And when he spotted Naina and me together, he got a motive.

The elevators in PGI don't open directly on to the wards. From straight and long corridors, there are perpendicular branches leading to the wards. The lifts open on to these. So by the time I turned into the corridor, Raana was nowhere in sight. Or perhaps that was him in the distance, a figure ducking into the ramp. I had been seen and recognized too.

As I spiraled down after him, I couldn't be sure if he went right down to ground floor, but that seemed the likely thing to do. By the time I emerged outside and my pupils adjusted to the sudden brightness of outdoors, I had lost the chase.

"*Kya hua daacter saab*?" The security at the exit was curious to see me emerge, my white overall flapping behind me, my steth hanging on for dear life to my neck. I asked him if he had seen someone run out before me. He hadn't. Then why are you wasting my time, you moron, I remember cursing mentally in my frustration.

I could now either go right towards Kairon Block and the hostels, or left towards the shops near the main gate or the gate itself. I went left, but he was not to be seen.

I returned to the guard and urged him to apply his mind. Didn't anyone precede me, hurrying if not running? Yes, a ward boy did seem to be in a hurry. Ward boy. So he was back to his old job, in more ways than one. Was he wearing a reddish shirt, I couldn't be sure if it was plain or had fine print, with dark pants? Yes, maybe he was.

Name?

No idea. Just know him by face.

Department? No luck.

I hoped the realization that he had been spotted and chased might have scared Raana into terminating his electronic correspondence. But no luck here either. That very night I heard from him again. This time too he had followed up his imagery, the video-clip of Naina and me near the car, with text. He did have low opinion of my cognitive powers.

'You and Dr. Naina having affair. That is why she killed her husband.'

She did not say it, although she had reason to do so two times over. Not only had she been right about Raana being the perpetrator of the mail, she was also the one amongst us four who had been most eager that we make sure Raana got his dues, and the most disappointed when we didn't. Yet she didn't say 'I told you so.' In fact she said nothing at all when I met her that evening. We were at her PC. I had intended to open my mail to show her the latest from Rajesh Suri alias Raana. But there was no need to take the trouble. Finally he had found her e- mail address too.

"Naina?"

"What does he want, Tara?" No demand for cash had been made. No attempt at blackmail. He was not doing it for money. Raana was out to ruin our peace of mind. That made it more disturbing, even frightening.

"Do you think he followed Kabir and me here?"

"I don't think so, Naina. I think it is the other way round.' The latter was more likely. After my last encounter with him at the JDH parking lot, there had been no more trouble from Raana. Chaaya had spotted him once at the pharmacy bang opposite CMC main gate. But he hadn't seen her, and neither did we see him again in the hospital or anywhere else for that matter. So why would he come to Chandigarh in Naina and Kabir's pursuit?

Only their presence again in the same hospital as him may have led him to make trouble for them. Perhaps he even reasoned that if he could get hold of something incriminating, he could blackmail them into silence about his shady history.

"What are we going to do? Shouldn't we call in the police now?"

"Not yet. First let me try and see if I can track him down him on my own. The security identified him as an employee."

As for tracing the mail, Sameer had come to a dead end like me. For pinning down the terminal or even the internet café from which the mail had originated, we needed to approach the service provider, who in turn may oblige only under orders from the cyber police. Sameer also offered to use his good offices with a certain inspector whose wife had benefited from the mastery of his scalpel. He had relieved her of her gall bladder and the nearly half a ton of stones it had been accumulating. The inspector and spouse still appeared faithfully for follow- up. But with no guarantee of the discretion of either the SP or the IP, we decided to skip both options till later.

"Don't you get the irony, Tara? In CMC he went scot-free because the authorities were too concerned about bad publicity. Now we are worrying about the same thing."

"Yes, but he's not getting away with it this time, Naina. I promise you this."

And I meant to keep it, whatever it took this time.

I don't know why it is that people in places of authority, people heading an organization, go into denial at the slightest suggestion of trouble. Maybe because the more problems they acknowledge, the more solutions they will have to come up with. Whatever may be the explanation, I have yet to meet a captain who, when informed that his ship may be sinking, would jump up and say 'Where is the problem? Show me. Let's see what can be done about it.'

Instead they go, 'Sinking? My ship? Impossible!'

Remember the Titanic?

Dr. Vinodh Pasricha, Medical Superintendent, PGI, was no less skeptical when I met him the next morning. I didn't tell him about the mails. Just what Raana had been caught doing in CMC Ludhiana, and that I had spotted him in this hospital.

"Are you sure he's the same person? Is he really working in PGI?"

As if it was all right if someone clicked nude pictures of patients as long as he was not a hospital employee. "Has he been doing the same here?"

Wasn't it a possibility, at the very least, I felt like asking him.

"What do you want me to do?"

For the last query, I had a definite answer. I wanted to go through the personnel records. It was unlikely that he was using his real name. Anyway I already knew him by two, Randeep Kakkar and Rajesh Suri. But personnel records would have his photograph; at least a xerox if not the original. I hoped to find his current name, address, anything to take me to the man. To rummage through employee details, I needed the sanction of the medical superintendent. Skeptical and reluctant he may have been, but the MS did not refuse me.

What was I going to do, once I traced him? Was I going to confront him, threaten him as he had done five years ago? You might well wonder if I had transformed into a fearless protagonist ready to take on the villain. Truth is, I did not have a definite plan of action. I don't know how, but somehow I hoped to get hold of his mobile which was sure to hold images and video clips of PGI patients now. One thing I was sure of. If I laid my hands on his cell again, this time I would not hand it over to the MS.

Mrs. Savita Garg was the head of personnel. In her fifties as someone in her position was likely to be, she was eager to oblige as someone in her post was unlikely to be. She did not seem to mind my intrusion into her domain or the extra burden of pulling out files of hundreds of Class IV employees, which of course her staff had to do. There was no separate section for ward boys, which meant I had to wade through files of safai wallahs, laboratory attendants, pharmacy assistants and many others.

I went through files of males employed after February 2004. Most had photographs, as they needed to submit photographic identity proofs, two-wheeler driving licenses, voter ID cards mostly. After six days of rummaging, which I could only do whenever I got a few moments of free time from my patients, I found 23 males between the ages of 20 and 40 who had not provided a photo ID.

"*Achha*? Let me see." Mrs. Garg was quite unbelieving of this lapse in her record keeping. All the offending files were from before she had joined a year and a half ago. "That Mr. Mehra!" She did not lose the opportunity to blame her predecessor. "He handed over so many incomplete records. I have been able to rectify only some of the deficiencies. I don't know what he did all day besides playing cards with the technicians." They were a regular sight, class III and IV employees of PGI, playing cards on the lawns in front of the paramedical blocks during winter months. I don't know where they set camp in summer.

Meanwhile, the personnel head had another idea. "You can try the SSHS." That was the staff and students health services. You had to submit photographs not only of yourself but also of your dependants to get free or subsidized medical care in PGI. That was a facility not many staff were likely to forego. So, after extracting a promise from the personnel head to let me know if her records turned up anything else, I proceeded to the SSHS with my list of 23 delinquents. Here the list dwindled to a mere 14. Fourteen men, seven of them ward boys, had not feel the need to open SSHS files. Raana had to be one of them. He was probably working in PGI as a ward boy, but I didn't rule out the possibility of Raana working in any other capacity.

I could go to the departments of these fourteen and enquire. But what was I supposed to ask? Does a fair man with black hair, about five feet four inches tall, who wears tight jeans with bright shirts when off duty, work in your department? That fitted the description of three out of five young middle class Punjabi men. Try as I might, I could not conjure up one distinguishing feature about Raana. No mole on the neck, no tattoo, no bushy eyebrows. Even Naina couldn't come up with anything, which meant that my poor observational skills were not to be blamed. That was the reason I was obsessed with getting my hands on his mug shot. This obsession was quickly becoming an impossible one. It was already a week since I had spotted Raana.

Meanwhile quirky advice came from an unexpected quarter. Sameer invited Naina, Smriti and me for dinner one Friday night. It was more to distract us than to celebrate his first wedding anniversary, though the end of the evening must have left him feeling ineffective in the former mission.

With our consent, his wife Madhu was privy to our troubles with the 'unprofessional' photographer. There should be no secrets between life-mates, after all. She must have given some thought to the matter because during dinner she offered her solution without warning.

"*Bhai saab*, if you don't mind can I give you a suggestion?"

Then without waiting to find out, she gave it.

"Why don't you get married? That will stop anyone of accusing you two of having an affair."

For a moment I had thought she was proposing a union between me and Naina. But she had more tact than that.

"Oh, come on Madhu," Sameer protested. "What a ridiculous idea! As if married men and women don't have affairs. How can he suddenly find a girl and get married, anyway?"

"Your parents must be searching for a bride for you by now, *nahin, bhai saab*? Your mother may be sending you some photographs even," she continued, ignoring her husband's interruption.

She was right really. Though no snapshots of eligible girls came by post for me, mother did bring up the topic whenever we talked on phone. She was in fact on the look out for a brother and sister duo for her daughter and son.

"How will it affect the accusation of murder, anyway?"

"With the motive on shaky grounds, that charge will not hold water either. Moreover, once this person Raana finds you carrying on with your life, he may feel his hold on you loosening and stop bothering you."

Actually it was sage reasoning from this college dropout from Ambala. Her family had considered Sameer too good a match to risk losing while she completed her graduation. So she had left college in the second year to tie the knot. Sameer had encouraged her to pursue her studies if she so wished, but she was content to run his household. Probably because of Naina's status as a widow with a child, she did not seem to consider the possibility of my romantic interest in her. Or maybe she did consider it but did not approve. She may even have been trying to steer me away from sin.

Sameer on the other hand very likely had an inkling of my feelings in the matter, though no word on the subject had passed between us. Perhaps that is why he was the strongest critic of his wife's proposition. But he too agreed we should try and ignore the mails.

"Just delete them right away without looking. He'll get frustrated and give up. I don't think he'll actually dare to make his accusation public. It's too flimsy anyway. You haven't replied to him, have you?"

"No, never. In fact he has no means of knowing we are giving any thought to his antics."

"Good. Then try not to."

And what of Naina? What was her reaction? I had sought her eyes when Madhu brought up matrimony. But at that very instant Smriti had commanded her attention and continued to do so till the topic was safely done with. But it was important for me to know how she took the prospect of my marrying someone else. As Taruni had said, she must have gauged my feelings towards her by now, whether or not she reciprocated them. So I broached the issue on the short drive home. She was dropping me this time. Sameer's house in Sector 11, all he had had to do was add a floor above his parent's, was close to PGI. In fact I had walked over on my way in.

"I hope you don't expect me to do as Madhu suggested. I'll do anything to get this maniac off our backs, but not this Naina. Not this."

"I'm sorry Tara. If I'd known this was on her mind, I would have warned you. But she never mentioned anything to me." Naina had been with Madhu since early evening helping her prepare the dinner spread.

"Eventually you'll marry, of course. But how can anyone be expected to find a girl and get married overnight?"

"Finding a girl is the easy part. Making her marry me is another story."

I couldn't believe I had said that. Surely she could not disregard my implication. But once again Naina managed to avoid displaying her reaction. She was either very good at it or plain lucky. She had just turned into my parking lot and a car backing out with the all too omnipresent Airtel jingle commandeered her concentration this time. After that it was only 'Bye Tara' and 'Goodnight Tara uncle' before her car drove out the gate.

There was another personnel section to be gone through. At Christian Medical College, Ludhiana. If nothing turned up here, we had decided to take our friends' advice, or some of it at least, to disregard the mails and videos and get on with life. But having already tried to wish away Raana without success four years ago, I wanted to follow every possible lead this time round.

The next day I applied half a day's leave and once again found myself in the office of the medical superintendent Brown Hospital, Ludhiana. Only this time the man on the chair was one Dr. Pramod Johnson, a fellow surgeon albeit a Urologist. He was more forthcoming than Dr. Joshi, perhaps because the offence had not taken place during his tenure. In any case, he readily granted me permission to peruse the records for Randeep Kakkar, Raana's official name in CMC.

This time at least I had a name. Hospital policy required records of personnel against whom disciplinary action, that included getting fired, had been taken, to be maintained for a minimum of ten years. His file was located in 25 minutes. But once again there was no photograph.

This couldn't have been a coincidence. There was a local address which I took down. There was no Randeep Kakkar or Raana or Rajesh Suri at number 38, Model Town. He was in Chandigarh, of course. The old man who opened the door had no idea of or interest in the previous occupants of the house. If at all Raana had actually inhabited it, ever. ❖

"Hello *beta*. We were just thinking of you." Brig Goraya was all enthusiasm as he greeted me at the door. It was a Sunday. I had stopped by at Naina's on my way back from Ludhiana. She had mentioned that her in-laws would be coming this week, but it had slipped my mind so that I was unprepared to have to wait for an opportunity to talk to her alone. We had naturally not shared the content of Naina's mailbox with them.

"Tara *beta*, if you are free we would like your help in an important matter."

He paused and looked at his wife and daughter-in law.

"We've decided to move to Chandigarh, so we can be with Naina and Smriti."

Move to Chandigarh. Be with Naina. Why? Why this sudden change of heart?

I tried to catch Naina's eye. Whose decision was it? Was this what she wanted?

You may recall I once mentioned third party was welcome. But that was a long time ago. Or was my increasing intimacy with their daughter- in -law making them uncomfortable? To give them credit, if they had any reservations in this direction, which most Indian parents or in-laws would have, they never let it show. I was always treated as one of the family. More like Naina's local guardian.

Meanwhile the Brigadier continued, "I've marked some

prospective houses up for sale in the classifieds. We would like to go and have a look. Do you mind coming along?" What he meant was, 'Do mind driving the car?'

Naina was on duty, so she could not accompany us. Smriti was to stay behind with Neelam. I snatched an opportunity to talk to Naina alone in the kitchen.

"What's up Naina? Why are they suddenly moving in?" She was in the process of pouring tea before we set out. She looked up, perplexed by my ill-concealed agitation.

"It's not sudden Tara. They have been meaning to do so for a while now."

"What about you? Are you happy with the arrangement?"

"Frankly Tara, I think you know me enough to realize I prefer to run my own show. But this is not about me. It's Smriti I have to think of. I'm sure it'll be much better for her to have her grandparents around rather than a maid for company all day."

Wouldn't a father be even better? The words were on the tip of my tongue when Mrs. Goraya came in to help with the tea.

Without another chance to talk to Naina, I found myself driving her in-laws around the city checking out residences for sale.

By lunch we had seen three flats in Mohali in addition to an independent house each in Panchkula and Chandigarh. Or I should say the Gorayas had seen. My mind was engaged elsewhere.

The Gorayas were moving in with Naina. They were disposing of their dream flat in NOIDA and setting up house here. Permanently. What if she decided to remarry? Me or someone else? What were they supposed to do then? Would they be comfortable living with their daughter-in-law's new husband? Was no one considering re-marriage as an option? Come on, Naina was a mere 31 years old. I had to stop them before they took the plunge. But here I was, helping them.

What could I say?

I had to talk to Naina. I had to find her alone. I would

do that as soon as we finished with this business and returned home. But when we did, Naina was missing. She was at the hospital. Any way it would take a minimum few months to even consider finalizing a deal. Before that I would talk to Naina and present my alternative.

But the Brigadier gave me much less time than that. "*Beta* I was wondering if you know of some good lawyer. There's a house we rather liked. Want to be sure the paperwork is in order."

Found a house. So soon? We had started house hunting on Sunday and it was only Friday. The military certainly trains you to think on your feet. There was no time to lose. I had to talk to Naina. I caught up with her in the pediatric intensive care.

"I have an exchange transfusion posted for 5.30, Tara. Give me a call around 6."

Once again we were alone in a doctors' duty room, this time of the operation theatre in Government Medical College, Chandigarh. She was sitting on one of the chairs updating a patient file.

"Tara, what are you doing here?" She looked up in surprise as I entered. I hadn't called her. Instead I had reached the pediatric ICU at 5.55 to be told she was in the OT to receive a caesarian baby. The latter had obviously not yet arrived. I had then proceeded to the theatre and changed into OT clothes with sufficient nonchalance to prevent any suspicion that I was not from GMC.

"What's up, Tara? Everything all right? You look all worked up." I was. My future and happiness depended on this moment.

"Naina, tell your father-in-law not to go ahead with the house deal."

"That's what you said over the phone. But why? Have you found out something about the owners? Something wrong with the papers?"

"No, no. It's not that. It's... you see, they need not move in with you. I mean you don't need them."

"Tara, I told you, I would rather manage on my own. But I think it's the best for Smriti. She'll have more family than I ever had."

"She could have a father instead. And the Gorayas need not move in."

Oh shit! Shit! As if circumstances were not sufficiently lacking in romance. In a duty room, both of us in shapeless OT greens. And now I was proposing a marriage of convenience.

"What?"

"What I mean to say, to ask you Naina," I went down on one knee of my pajama, "Will you marry me? Not to provide Smriti with a father or to save her grandparents the trouble of shifting. I want you to marry me because I love you. Have done so since I don't know when..."

The odds were already against her saying yes to such a proposal at such a time. Wouldn't it confirm what Raana was accusing us of? Wouldn't it be the worst thing we could do right now, like putting a noose around our necks? I was prepared for so many objections, but not for the one that she raised when she did speak.

"So Chaaya was right. You ditched her because you had a crush on me." Chaaya did know.

"Did she say that? That I ditched her?" I was still on the floor while she had stood up.

"Not in as many words. But she did say that you never truly loved her, that your heart was elsewhere. That's why she opted out."

I got up too. "That's not fair. How come I don't know what she felt? When did she have this heart to heart with you?"

"She calls up now and then." I never thought Chaaya capable of this, of maligning me long-distance. I had not heard from her after she relayed the news of Smriti's birth. But I had not called her either, so I was not complaining about that.

"Did she tell you I begged her not to go to Meerut to see that guy? Did she tell you I offered to talk to her parents, even to accompany her to Meerut to do so? Did she tell you that?"

"No Tara, but you yourself said that much just now, that you don't know for how long you have... had feelings for me."

We were standing face to face in the middle of the room by now. I put my hands on her shoulders, and I'm not sure but maybe I shook her too.

"All right. Yes. Maybe I was attracted to you while we were in Ludhiana. So what? What is so wrong in that? We can't always decide how we feel. But we can decide how we act. Tell me Naina, tell me one instance when I made my feelings apparent. Have I ever...what do they say, made a pass at you?"

"Tara!"

I was completely out of control by now. "Or do you think I killed Kabir so I could have you, Naina? Is that what you think of me?"

I deserved it. To be slapped in the face by the woman I adored. Everything had led to it; the timing, the place, the reason I first suggested for matrimony. And I had thought my life was already a mess.

She kept her word. Mrs. Savita, the Personnel head of PGI.

"One of the ward boys from the Obstetrics and Gynecology ward has not reported for work since the fifth of the month," she called to say. Fifth! That was the day after I saw Raana at the elevator! And Obstetrics and Gynecology was certainly his favorite place in the hospital.

I was in her office between patients in the OPD.

"Can I have his particulars? Name, address, whatever."

"He's one Ramesh Kumar"

Ramesh Kumar. I checked my list of 14 potentials. He was on it. He could be Raana. Randeep Kakkar in CMC Ludhiana, Ramesh Kumar in PGI Chandigarh, the initials were the same. Rajesh Suri on the net. The R was still common.

"Can I go through his file?"

"Sure, doctor."

Age 33. Single. Joined PGI in June 2004. That fit. Previous job in a hospital in Jallandhar. That didn't, but he was not likely to risk anyone checking out his credentials at CMC Ludhiana. So it was probably a fake testimonial from some hospital in Jallandhar. There was only one address, both under temporary and permanent category. I copied it down before heading for the Obs and Gyne ward.

The sister-in-charge of the ward was out for tea. A junior nurse was holding fort. It was her first week in the ward and she knew nothing about Ramesh Kumar. There were some other nurses and ward staff going about their duties, but I did not wish the entire ward to know I had come asking about Ramesh, so back I went to the plastics OPD for the time being.

It was past three before I could get out of the OPD. This time Mrs. Blessy George was back at the nurses' station of the Obs and Gyne ward. "Ramesh Kumar. Yes, yes. He's our ward boy. He's absent since fifth September. He didn't apply for leave. Didn't send in a leave letter either. Normally he's a good sincere boy. I don't know why he's absconding without informing."

Maybe I do.

"Behaviour? No complaints. He's a good worker. Quite smart also. Always asking questions about medicines."

Like Lepirudin.

"His looks? Fair, about five feet five or six, you know, medium height. Must be between thirty and thirty-five."

It could be Raana.

The big brass padlock on the door of flat number 82, Ground Floor, Sector - 7B was more or less what I had anticipated. In fact I was prepared for worse. I had half expected the address to be fictitious. But I suppose that would not be easy to pull of for a Government employee.

It was not yet seven in the evening but the days were getting shorter already, and it was getting to be dark. I climbed the staircase to the first floor and rang the bell of the flat right above Ramesh Kumar's. A woman answered but did not unlatch the chain which prevented the door from opening fully.

Not having nursed much hope of finding the address, I had failed to give sufficient thought to the matter of my introduction. So I had to literally think on my feet. A doctor from PGI come looking for a missing ward boy was not likely to hold water. I decided to pass off as someone from the Personnel Department of PGI, keeping my designation vague. The lady looked to be about thirty herself, probably a housewife waiting for her spouse to return from work. She looked me up and down and I think she did not buy my impersonation because she did not open the door any further. Still, though I did not win her trust, I got the information I had come looking for, because she willingly answered my queries.

She confirmed it was Ramesh Kumar who lived downstairs. He lived alone, except for a few months each year when his parents stayed with him. He had been working in PGI since the last three or four years. That's when he had shifted to this current flat and that's how far their acquaintance went. She had no clue as to where and what he had been before moving in. He was not the socializing type she informed me, kept mostly to himself. Or maybe to his camera and computer.

According to her, Ramesh's absence from work was due to a death in the family, in Patiala. I think she said it was his uncle's son who had died in an accident.

As for the omission of a leave application, she naturally could not enlighten me there.

"I don't know about that. He left in a hurry. What do you expect?" she reasoned in Hindi.

I didn't argue with her about the existence of such means of communication as telephones and cell phones.

Neither did I see it fit to ask her to describe his appearance. I was supposed to know what he looked like. Physical description was not helping my investigation anyway.

I thanked her for her cooperation and took my leave.

It could be Raana. If it was, he sure was keen to avoid me.

That was all I could accomplish after a day's detective work. None of the leads ruled out the possibility that Ramesh Kumar was another alias for Raana. None clinched it either. I had to have his Photograph.

I didn't see Naina for a full week after my disastrous proposal. Thankfully, I didn't see any mail from Raana either. Perhaps he knew he had achieved more than he had set out to do. Not that I was sulking after the slap. It was work that kept me away from Sector 32. And what I wished to say to her now was not to be said over the phone. Or in a hospital gown. I was determined not to mess it up this time. But I was also aware the longer we put off talking, the more awkward it would be. Naina felt so too, I think.

"Hello Tara." Somehow she was always the one to re-establish contact after a break, even if it was a short one this time. She was calling from my campus. She had just finished some work in the PGI library. Was I free to see her before she left?

It was about four thirty on a Friday afternoon. I was on evening rounds with my team. In fact my cell had been on silent mode and the only reason I answered when I noticed the blue light blinking, was because it was from her. Had I left her call unanswered, she may have taken it as a rebuff. So I excused myself from the rounds much to my professor's displeasure, and hurried to the library building.

She was waiting outside on the steps, looking radiant in a lemon yellow salwar kameez. Just a week without seeing her, and my heart skipped a beat as I drew near enough to inhale her now familiar perfume.

"Do you have your library card with you?"

"Oh, so that's why you called me!" I said in mock disappointment. "I carry it with me all the time so I can use it for my friends in an emergency," I continued, encouraged by her smile. I think both of us were relieved that the meeting was not as awkward as we had feared.

After getting the journals that she had selected issued on my card, I drove her homewards. Another reason for calling me, I teased her, was free transport. She had come to PGI with a colleague from GMC, but their timing for the return trip did not tally, so I undertook the task.

"Naina," I began soon as I hit Madhya Marg. "There's something I want to say to you."

"Tara, I'm sorry about that day in the OT. I don't know what came over me."

"It's OK. I did get carried away. I know this not a good time for us. I should have been less desperate." I slowed to let a honking Ford overtake us, and then continued.

"Anyway, what I want to say is, don't take any decision in a hurry. Had it been some other time and place, had not Raana sent those mails, had Chaaya not accused me of dumping her, would you have responded differently? No, no, don't answer me now. Think about it. Do this much for me. If it's still a 'No,' then believe me, I will not repeat last Friday's performance. So don't go cold on me. I don't want you to lose a good friend."

Wow! I was calm enough to crack a joke, and she to smile.

"Seriously, as you know, I do have some experience in getting over the women in my life. Maybe I'll take Madhu's advice and marry a beautiful Kangra girl, after all."

This time I wasn't joking. I didn't believe in one-way relationships either. I didn't believe in pursuing a girl till her 'no' became a 'yes'. I expected my partner to bring in the same passion or at least commitment to the alliance.

"It does seem the sensible thing to do. To marry a wonderful friend who wants me with all my baggage, who I know will cherish my daughter as his own. It would be the most practical thing to do rather than face life alone. Only problem is Tara, it wouldn't be fair. It wouldn't be fair to you. Because I would be doing it for convenience, not for love. I'm sorry Tara, but that's an emotion I don't feel for you. Or will ever feel, for you or anyone else."

I didn't say anything like, 'Marry me anyway. You'll gradually learn to love me.'

What was one supposed to do till then? Live like brother and sister? Or do the marital duty anyway? Much as I adored her, or maybe because I loved her so, I wanted Naina to love me back or not at all.

"And if I can't love the sweetest guy who's been a wonderful friend, I don't think I have it in me any more."

"Don't shut any doors Naina, not permanently. Tell you what, let's just forget about this whole episode. Let's see how we feel once things settle down. I only hope you won't regret when I marry my Himachali beauty!

She turned and punched me lightly in the chest for that. I barely resisted the urge to grab her hand and kiss those slender fingers one by one. ❖

At three, Smriti had yet to have a birthday party. This September 30th Naina was determined to give her one.

'I don't want to deny her more than what fate has already deprived her of'

But the poor child almost missed it this year too.

I was on call, so I phoned to wish her, only to learn from Neelam that Naina had taken her to the emergency department of GMC. It was one of the dogs hanging around the faculty flats, neither a stray nor a pet. An ophthalmologist's wife took great pride in feeding the strays with her kitchen leftovers, encouraging them to hang around the faculty houses.

"If she's so fond of dogs, why doesn't she keep them in her house? Or at least get them vaccinated. What if they bite someone? She thinks she's such a great animal lover." Naina had chafed once, angrier than I had ever seen her except of course on the day she slapped me.

Smriti had stepped too close to one of the mongrels while it was devouring Mrs. Gupta's, the eye specialist's spouse, stale chicken biryani. The dog growled and tried to attack, causing the petrified girl to trip and hit her head on the edge of a scooter parked nearby.

I met mother and daughter only a day after the incident. I had talked to Naina on her mobile but Smriti had already received four stitches on the forehead by then.

'No need to come. Things are under control,' Naina informed me. This time they really were, thank god.

I found the little patient with a bandage round her head. "Happy birthday, my brave buttercup." I handed her a doll I'd bought after much indecision over whether or not she was too old for it. Wish Taruni had married and given me some experience with nieces and nephews.

"My birthday was yesterday, Tara uncle. Mummy promised a party," She pointed out. Canine attack, emergency department, four stitches, all were forgotten. What was bothering her was the party which once again never took place.

I decided to try my hand at fulfilling the dear child's wish. "What did you do with all the food Naina? Can't we have the party today?"

"Everything is there, dumped in the fridge. But we'll have to contact everyone again. I'm not up to it Tara. Besides I'm on call. Had her Daada-Daadi been able to stay on, they could have pitched in."

The Gorayas had left by the afternoon Shatabdi two days ago, before Smriti's mishap. They would have liked to be present for their grand-daughter's birthday celebration, but Mrs. Goraya's niece was getting married in Ghaziabad, and the bride's mother had laid claim to her sister's presence at the wedding. As for their plans of moving base, there was no more talk of it for the time being. The deal which had driven me to desperation had fallen apart on its own.

"Neelam and I will manage if you have to go."

Naina finally relented, called up the guest list again, which was mostly made of offspring of fellow GMCites. Most of them did turn up at such short notice and were happy to have a party after all. Despite a cake with a wedge missing, the not-so-crisp-any-longer vegetable puffs and the not cold 'cold' drinks which had found no place in the overflowing fridge, it was a happy evening at least for the birthday girl and her young friends.

Not that it was unhappy for the rest of us. Except that Kabir's absence was expected to be felt on the first birthday party of his child. Also to be expected was the awkwardness between Naïna and myself. Despite our attempt to clear the air, it was not to disappear overnight. So while the kids played musical chairs, ate their cake and left the puffs, burst the balloons, the adults went through the motions of a party each carrying his or her own emotional baggage, mine miniscule in comparison to the mother. Naina was not summoned to the hospital in the midst of the party. Thank god for small mercies.

The party was over. Smriti was sleeping. Neelam was clearing up the mess left behind by two dozen brats. Naina asked me to stay back for coffee, which we stood sipping in her balcony.

"Thanks Tara. You made Smriti's day."

"She's welcome."

"I didn't know you could manage a bunch of kids so well."

"Does that make you want to change your mind?"

Seconds passed as I held my breath. "Just kidding, hope I'm allowed to do that?"

She smiled and I exhaled. She straightened up and one hand went involuntarily to her lower back. It had been a long day.

"Your back troubling you? Why don't you sit on the swing? It can take at least one of us." I suggested.

"Actually it's meant for two," she said as she sat down without meeting my eyes.

Something in the downward gazing head told me my life was about to change forever. I sat down beside her on the swing. Two could fit on it. Snugly.

"Chand, there's a confession I have to make. Maybe two."

I'm not sure exactly when she had stopped calling me that, but the revival of my nickname could be a good omen.

I waited, afraid to interrupt.

"Chaaya didn't really accuse you of dumping her. She didn't accuse you of anything. In fact she said pretty much the same as you, that you yourself may have been unaware of your ... err... feelings for me. And she didn't tell me this to turn me against you. Rather the opposite."

Good old Chaaya. I should have known better than to believe otherwise.

"And the second one?"

I glanced sideways at her while she continued to keep herself busy with the coffee mug in her hand.

"What I said about not loving you… tell me Chand, wouldn't you rather marry someone who's not a widow and has a daughter?"

"No."

"Someone younger for whom you would be the first and only man in her life?"

"No."

"It seems a poor deal for you to have me with Smriti and my past."

"Haven't you heard of package deals? You were saying something about loving me?"

"Not loving you. I mentioned not loving you."

That was an ability we shared, to retain a sense of humour at the most awkward moments.

"What about it?"

"I think that's not entirely true either."

Not loving you. Not true. Two negatives made a positive. Was she telling me she loved me? My poor heart was going from atrial fibrillation into ventricular arrhythmia.

"It's just that I feel guilty about thrusting myself and Smriti on you."

"Guilty. Guilty. I'm done with feeling guilty, Naina. Enough for the two of us. That's all I've been doing ever since I realized what you mean to me. I've been sick with it. But not any more. What is so wrong in loving? I didn't hurt any one, at least I didn't mean to." Chaaya was not so easily forgotten. "And you? Don't you think you deserve another chance at living?"

"Don't you think *you* deserve better?"

"Better than the woman I love?"

We had been sitting rather stiffly on the unmoving swing looking ahead or down, anywhere but at each other.

I finally turned towards her, took the coffee mug from

her, put it down in one of her potted plants, and took both her hands in mine.

"No really Chand, doesn't it bother you that I've been married, have a child?"

"That you are not a virgin? Isn't that what you really want to ask, Naina?"

She looked away and I was afraid I had succeeded in offending her once again. But she didn't pull her hands away.

"I never planned this, Naina. I never even thought about my preferences, married or single, virgin or not. I ... I just know I think of you all the time Naina, 24X7. And that I would like to spend the rest of my days proving that God did plan you to be happy eventually. As for Smriti, how could you suggest she would be unwanted baggage?"

"She adores you. Did I tell you she plans to marry her dear Tara Uncle when she grows up?"

"In that case you had better do so before she beats you to it!"

"What about your Himachali girl?"

"I'm afraid she'll have to be content with someone else."

I turned her face towards mine and did what I had been dreaming of for so long. I pushed her hair aside from her forehead and kissed her there, on her eyelids, then on her nose and finally I kissed her lips. She kept her eyes down as I pulled back to look at her. I lifted her chin and claimed that sweet mouth once again. What had begun as a tentative coming together of the lips now turned into a release of the longing that had been long buried deep within. When she turned to hide her face in my neck, I kissed her cheek, her ear, her hair. ❖

CHAPTER 11

It was nearly midnight by the time I could pull myself away from my newfound life. Instead of simply hitting the bed and dreaming sweet dreams, I opened my mail. We had not heard from Raana for some time now, so he was not on my mind. But I was on his. There was mail from Rajesh Suri sitting in my inbox. I almost decided not to open it. I was reluctant to contaminate this night. But I did open it, and I can still feel the tremor in my fingers on the mouse and the palpitations in my chest that the contents gave me. It was a video of the very moment I had been afraid of spoiling. Of our first kiss. Our first embrace. In Naina's balcony not two hours ago. Where had Raana been?

"What's up Tara?"

I was back in Naina's house as fast as I could drive without being pulled up for over-speeding. I went to the balcony where we had met bliss not long ago and looked around, expecting to find what? Hidden cameras?

"What are you doing Tara?" she asked again. She had a sleeping Smriti in her arms. "I'll just put her in bed."

"Can Neelam take care of her for a while? I need to talk to you."

"Neelam is not here."

"But she was here in the evening."

"She left after finishing her work. We were in the balcony..."

"Doesn't she inform you when she's leaving?"

"She normally does. But sometimes when I'm busy, like putting Smriti to bed, she simply goes off. It's a self-locking door, you know. Yesterday she'd already taken permission for the night off. She may not have wanted to disturb us." A faint blush colored her cheeks.

"For how long have you had her?

"Ever since we moved in. She had been working for the family who stayed here before us, and they recommended her. Why are you asking so many questions about her?"

"Because Neelam is Raana's cameraman or woman."

"What!"

I told her about the latest video from Raana. "Who else could have filmed us Naina?" Naina's balcony faced away from the rest of the faculty flats. It overlooked the road beyond which was the Sector 32 Park. There was no way someone from outside the building could have done the shooting unless armed with a telescopic camera. In any case we were facing the camera bang on. The only place to get that shot from was Naina's bedroom which opened on to the balcony. Anyone in the darkened room would have been invisible and free to capture us on camera through the partially open door.

"Do you know where she stays?"

"With a family, some Sandhus, in Sector 7."

"Sector 7!" That was where Ramesh Kumar stayed.

"I still don't think she can do this Tara." I wouldn't have thought so too. She had seemed decent enough. The usual story. Drunkard husband. Two small kids. A boy, five or six years old, who sometimes accompanied her and kept Smriti entertained for hours. A daughter living with some relations in Kullu. She lived in a small outhouse of a big bungalow working for the occupants of the house before and after she finished her chores at Naina's.

Then again, was it so surprising that a person in her position had succumbed to the temptation to supplement her meager resources? Be it as it may, right then I was in no mood for justifying her betrayal

"Does she have a camera phone?"

"Who doesn't these days? Wait a minute. She changed her phone just a couple of weeks ago! And this one is a real fancy one with a 5 mega pixels camera, I think."

"Start looking for a new maid."

"But her things? She didn't take all her stuff."

"I'm sure Mr. Raana will compensate her adequately."

"Oh Tara this is becoming a bit scary.'

"A bit? It scared the shit out of me to think there's a mole inside your house. I feel as if the whole mess is getting out of hand. We've sat on it long enough. Or I should say I, because you wanted to go to the police right from the start. Tomorrow I'm going to do just that. Meanwhile, I don't care how it looks, but there's no way I'm leaving you alone tonight. So if you give me a sheet and a pillow, I'll be quite comfortable on your sofa."

It was already past eight when I found myself back in PGI. I had had very little sleep in the night. No, no, I did lie down chastely like a good Indian guy in Naina's drawing room, while she and Smriti occupied their bedroom. Our minds were too full of Raana to make better use of the night, at any rate. Or to sleep soundly, for that matter. The night had all but passed before I had managed to catch a wink. By then it was time to get up. At six-thirty Naina tried to revive us both with cups of ginger-flavoured tea. She had tossed and turned the night away too. While she went about the business of getting ready, I kept Smriti out of trouble. As for breakfast, only the little girl had an appetite for one. Finally, I dropped the daughter at a friend's who would look after her till Naina returned, and the mother at the Hospital, for her morning rounds. Neelam did not report back for work, of course.

So when I want to meet the Police, whom do I go to? Just walk into the nearest Police Station? That had not helped much in the past. I took up Sameer's offer of going through his Inspector friend to get an appointment with the law enforcers. He fixed up a 10am appointment with none less than the Inspector General of Police. Lay it all out before him. That's what I would do now. Let the law take its course. The Media could have their day too.

Meanwhile, it was time to shave, shower, and maybe breakfast, if I felt calm enough for the last. The prospect of meeting the IG made me more than a little edgy. Then I had to do my ward rounds. That shouldn't take long. It was 2nd October, Gandhi Jayanti, one of the rare days in a year when PGI Out Patient Departments are closed and formal ward rounds are replaced with a quicker inspection.

I had my mandibles nicely lathered when the phone rang. It was Sameer calling from his cell.

"Hi! Are you on campus? Will you do me a favor, man? There's a ruptured aortic aneurysm in the emergency. Can you go and manage? Got an emergency of my own. It's Dad. He's complaining of chest pain so we are on our way to cardiology. Will fill in the details when I see you."

"No problem. I'll handle it. You take care of uncle."

I looked at my watch. It was 8.30. A vascular repair could take hours. Sameer knew of my impending meeting. Obviously he had no other option. If I didn't help out, precious time would be lost trying to contact someone else. The delay could cost the patient his life. An aneurysm is a dilatation of an artery. This one was in the aorta, a major artery. And it had ruptured. It wouldn't take long for the patient to bleed to death.

I was in the OT and scrubbed by 8.55. The patient was already on the table and prepared, ready for the knife. The rupture was in the abdominal part of the aorta, just below where the renal arteries branch out from it. It didn't look good. The aneurysm was more than 6cm in diameter. Why the patient was not already dead from loss of blood was the stuff of medical miracles.

It took me and my Senior Resident all of three hours to repair the aorta using a Dacron tube graft. Sameer turned up sometime during the surgery.

"Thanks Tara. I owe you one. It was angina, thank god. No infarction this time. Dad's had a bypass you know. I'd already made him keep his Nitroglycerine under the tongue and the pain was gone by the time we reached cardiology. He's all right for now. I dropped him back home."

"No sweat Sameer. But this aorta doesn't look good to me. Just have a look."

Sameer scrubbed and offered to take over. But having started the repair, I did not wish to abandon the task half done. In fact on any other day I would have considered myself lucky to get this case. It was an unusual one. Aortic aneurysms are generally seen in elderly men, over sixty years of age. Once they rupture the prognosis is not so good. Many die before reaching a hospital while still others succumb to post-op complications. This patient was only thirty four. We were hopeful youth would improve his chances of survival.

So it was only after I had put the last suture into the artery that I handed the patient over to Sameer to close the abdomen.

By then I *was* tired, dirty and hungry. So I asked for the patient's file, entered my operation notes and left the patient in Sameer's custody. I had already missed the 10am appointment. Fortunately, Sameer had not forgotten about it. Between driving his father to and from PGI, he had let the officer know, apologized for my absence, and rescheduled the meeting to four in the evening at the IG's residence. But bath and breakfast eluded me still.

I had just pulled out the phone from my pocket to let Naina know about the rescheduled visit to the IG, when it rang. It was another friend, Suresh, calling from Ludhiana. He had some good news, if anything to do with Raana could be called that. Anyway, Suresh had succeeded where I had not. He had traced out Raana's photograph. He looked where I did not, which now seemed such an obvious place to look for a photograph, the photography section of CMC.

"I thought there might be a copy of the photograph taken for his ID card if shot in the Photo section," Suresh told me. Most employees got themselves shot by the hospital photographer for their identity cards. Some chose to supply their own.

"There wasn't any ID photo, but guess why his mug shot was there on the computer? He had received the Employee of the Year Award on Republic Day!"

A handful of hospital employees are nominated each year to receive these awards from the administration in recognition of their 'good work.' Raana got his in January 2002. I don't know if phone cameras were available then, but Employee of the Year. Raana!

"Can you believe it? Raana, a model worker. What a joke. Anyway, I've got his snap on a CD. I'm in the ward right now. Will mail it to you as soon as I hit my PC."

I had it in when I reached mine. Now that I was in possession of his portrait, I decided to pick up the thread of my amateur investigations starting with the sister-in-charge of private ward. Maybe I could give the police their criminal on a platter after all, when I went to meet the IG.

"I'm at the bus stand Doctor, waiting for a bus to Jallandhar," Sister Blessy informed me a few minutes later. She was making use of the Mahatma's birthday to attend a wedding in the City of Sports Goods. If I could make it to the Sector 22 bus stand before her bus departed, she would have a look at the photograph and I would know whether Ramesh Kumar and Raana were one and the same person, which by now I had come to believe was true. I needed her to confirm. But she could not promise to miss her bus for my sake.

So once again I was driving out in my car, cursing the speed limit of '55 kmph for light vehicles,' too prominently displayed along the roads to feign ignorance. I have never considered myself an extraordinarily lucky or unlucky fellow. But when it came to Raana, I was beginning to think I was jinxed. As I parked the car and rushed towards the Jallandhar booth, even before I reached it I could sense the emptiness which immediately follows the departure of a bus or train to be filled again for the next one. I looked around hoping Sister Blessy had deemed the matter significant enough to miss one bus for which was really not such a big deal, with one bus leaving for her destination every 20 minutes. But no, the typical Bollywood scene where the heroine is found waiting at the platform or departure lounge after the train or plane has left was not to be. Mrs. Blessy was not to be seen. A call from her mobile confirmed she was 'so sorry, but could not wait.'

I abandoned the thought of revisiting Raana's Sector 7 residence, not wanting to scare him away in case he did decide to return to it. ❖

CHAPTER 12

Breakfast time had come and gone without any nourishment finding its way into my body. After the cake and puff from Smriti's party yesterday evening, I had not eaten anything solid. My body suddenly brought this fact to my notice by initiating contractions in my stomach and tremors in my fingers. Not feeling fit to drive back, I decided to eat at one of the dhaabas opposite the bus stand.

But it was not time for that yet. After ordering aloo paranthas, I had just sipped the water from a tumbler of dubious microbiological content, when a certain feminine voice made me look at a table across the room. The table was about ten meters from mine, towards the interior of the dimly lit dhaaba. She was sitting with her back to me but I had no doubt who it was. I had seen and heard her enough to be sure it was Neelam. Naina and I had decided not to pursue her in the hope that, unaware that his mole had been discovered, Raana may try to use her again.

I busied myself with my phone when she got up to leave with her companion, a man about Raana's age and size, but no it was not Raana. Still I thought it would be worthwhile following them, so when I spied them heading towards the parked two-wheelers, I went for my car. She mounted the pillion and he sped off, with me on his trail. He turned left from the roundabout towards Kiran Theatre and turned into the parking next to it. Both alighted and headed towards, oh no, not the Rehri Market. The Sector 22 Rehri Market is a maze of small stalls. It would be impossible to keep them in sight. So instead of following them in, I hung about the Bajaj Pulsar. They were bound to come back to it sooner or later. I only wished it would be sooner.

"Namaste Bhaiyaji! Aap yahan? Kisi ka wait *kar rahe ho?* I nearly choked on the vegetable puff I had been devouring hungrily in lieu of the meals which were eluding me from morning. She looked quite guileless, actually seeming pleased to see me. Was she really innocent, or was she an accomplished actor? It was only last night that she had been busy intruding our most private moment. How could she even look me in the eye?

Had they spotted me at the *Dhaaba* after all? Now she was alone. There was no sight of her escort. Neither did she make any move towards the parked motorcycle which she had ridden not long since. I could not possibly ask about her companion without giving myself away. Should I confront her with her role in the clandestine photography? Or should I stick to our original plan of feigned ignorance?

I chose the latter and asked her whether she was here on an errand for Naina. There was only a passing uncertainty in her features before she smiled brightly and said she had the day off. Would report for work tomorrow. We'll see when tomorrow comes, or rather we will not see you, you liar.

"Didi ko miloge to mera namaste kehna," was her parting line as I walked away, being left with no other option. Nothing to show for standing around for more than an hour at the parking lot.

It was nearing three in the afternoon. An hour to go. I decided to take a look at my patients, including that morning's ruptured aorta. I wanted to see how he was doing. After that, time permitting, I could even go to the private ward and try my luck with the nurses on duty there. With Raana's photograph, maybe someone would confirm he and Ramesh Kumar were one and the same. So I proceeded to the recovery room.

"The aortic aneurysm case that came in the morning? He was declared dead half an hour ago. He had a cardiac arrest," I was informed at the nurses' station.

He didn't make it after all.

"Can I see his file, if its still here?" One of the nurses looked for the file on the counter. As she pulled it out from under a pile, a large brown envelope fell on to the floor.

"Ravi." She called out to the ward boy. "Why is this still here. Didn't you give it to the relatives?"

"*Koi nahin hai. Ek tha, bhai ya pata nahin kaun, woh bhi gayab ho kgaya.* File *mein koi* address *bhi nahin hai.*" The fellow replied in Hindi. There was no relative with the patient. One gentleman of unknown relation had been around, but he too was not to be seen now. There was no address on his file either. What a sad end. No loved one at the deathbed. No one to claim the remains.

"Then send his things to the morgue with the body," the nurse instructed the ward boy.

Something slipped out of the folder when it was lifted up from the floor. Since it fell near my feet, I bent down and retrieved it. At the same time as I extended my arm to pass it over, I happened to glance at what I held in my hand. I pulled my hand back and took another look. There was no mistaking the face I had been looking for. It was Raana. It was a wallet which had opened and fallen face down of the floor. On the inside was a photograph. It was the same snapshot which Suresh had mailed me this morning. Of Raana receiving an award at a CMC Republic Day function. The presenter had been snipped away, preserving only Raana's grinning visage. For weeks I had been trying to get hold of Raana's photograph. Today, within the span of a few hours I was confronting it for the second time.

"Is this the patient?" Or I should have asked *was* the patient.

The file proclaimed him to be one Narinder Pal. The nurse took a look at the card and nodded in affirmation. But I needed to be hundred percent sure.

"Where's the body?"

Sent to the morgue, where else? The nurse seemed both surprised and impatient at my sudden animation and interest in a dead patient. "Ravi, has the body been shifted?" she questioned the ward boy again.

I didn't wait for his answer but hurried to bed number 27, noticing the number that was written in black felt pen on his file cover. But bed umber 27 was empty. Meanwhile, Ravi came up behind me to confirm the body had just been taken to the mortuary. This was outside the main hospital building near the old bank and the staff parking lot.

I rushed towards the corridor. The elevator doors closed as I neared it. Two cracked soles peeped out from under a body covered with a white sheet. Once again I rushed down the ramp in pursuit of Raana. Only this time it was his body I was after. I was in time to meet the trolley as it came out of the elevator on the ground floor. I held my breath as they lifted the sheet.❖

CHAPTER 13

I had spent almost the entire day running around town trailing people looking for this one person. And he had been here all along, literally under my nose. I had operated upon him in the morning and then left him to search for him. I had even tried to save his life, unaware that he was the one making mine miserable. Now I was seeing the lifeless face of the man who had tormented me for the last six weeks. He had also had me stabbed four years ago, but compared to the mental agony of the recent weeks, that offence appeared minor.

I should have been relieved, elated even, to see the last of Raana. Not a very charitable reaction, I know. He was a fellow human being and all that. Not more than a few minutes ago, I had actually felt pity for this same person, pity for his lonely, untimely, uncared for death. Pity I do feel for him, still. Not just for the way he died, but also for the way he lived his life. Coasting from hospital to hospital gathering obscenities on camera. Nowhere where I had probed, did anyone call Raana or Randeep his 'friend.' Although he had been popular enough at the work place, his personal life drew a blank everywhere I looked. Not just his deathbed, his life had been loveless too, as far as I could fathom. Neither were there any signs of wealth accumulated. I don't believe profiteering was his driving force in any case. It was more of a mental aberration, an obsession, which made him do what he did. It was the last thing he accomplished in fact, uploading the video from Neelam's mobile on to a computer and mailing it to us.

I lay no undue claim to benevolence. I did not feel sorry for him the instant I saw him dead. That came only later, on reflection and retrospection. Yet the relief, the elation, were missing too. Instead, what I felt was frustration. Unaware that I was on the wrong track all along, it had finally seemed like I was closing in on Raana. I had actually started looking forward to a confrontation with him, to giving him a piece of my mind before the law took over. I had already begun to imagine Raana behind bars and to derive a certain satisfaction from the image. But Raana had escaped retribution. He was beyond the reach of earthly law.

There was also a sense of disappointment in the realization that I had been chasing an illusion. Raana was not Ramesh Kumar. He was not a PGI employee after all, even though he managed to pass as one. I knew of at least one security guard who had been mistaken.

And then there was doubt. If I was so mistaken about Raana being Ramesh, what if I was also wrong about Raana being the perpetrator of the clandestine photography and the mails. What if they were two different people? While Raana, Randeep Kakkar and Narinder Pal were one and the same person, there was no evidence that Rajesh Suri was one of his many pseudonyms too. We had not determined anything to link Rajesh Suri the e-mailer to Raana the photographer of nude patients. I had spotted him in PGI and jumped to conclusions. His evasion of me that day did not prove a thing either. He would naturally wish to avoid anyone privy to his unsavory past, especially if that person had also provided target practice for his crony's knife.

There was also the matter of his knowledge of medicines, disproportionate to his capacity as a ward boy. We had tried to rationalize it by crediting him with intelligence and inquisitiveness beyond his position. Was it really possible for a ward boy to understand enough about Lepirudin to claim it as a purported poison?

Did we have the right person or was there someone else out there, still free to shadow us? How were we to know?

Even in life Raana had been a ghost, a shadow. For weeks we had been trying in vain to trace him, to discover his true identity, who he really was. And now he was dead. All we had was a body and a multitude of names. The last one, Narinder Pal, had been provided by Raana himself even as he had been brought writhing in pain to the hospital. Was it his true name then? The one he had divulged so close to his end like a dying declaration? I am only guessing here. Except for the photograph and some loose change, there had been no papers in his wallet. No identity card, no driving license, no letters. No nothing. If Sameer had not called me that day, if his father had not had angina, we would never have known that Raana was dead.

There was nothing to do now except wait. Wait and pray for the mails and the photography to die out with the man.

Meanwhile, maybe justice had been done after all. Maybe he went to hell.

One thing I *was* thankful for through this ordeal called Raana. I was grateful for my ignorance in the operating theatre that morning. For not knowing the patients' identity when I operated on him. He had been under general anesthesia with a mask covering part of his face when I entered the scene. The senior resident had already prepared him for surgery. I had simply opened his abdomen and sutured his blood vessel. The name Narinder Pal on his file naturally did not hold any meaning for me. After the surgery I had handed him over to Sameer.

Had I recognized him there and then on the OT table, what would I have done? I am a doctor, ethically, morally, even legally bound to save lives. How sincerely would I have been able to apply myself to save this one? Sincerely enough I hope, but I'll never know. I am glad to be spared at least this dilemma. ❖

L.G 24210

Acknowledgements

I am grateful to Sunil K Poolani of Leadstart Publishing for his informal and friendly mails. They provided a comfort level which made the bringing out of this book as enjoyable as it was exciting.